LILLIAN BECKWITH

A Shine of Rainbows

Illustrated by Douglas Hall

ARROW BOOKS

Arrow Books Limited
17-21 Conway Street, London W1P 6JD

An imprint of the Hutchinson Publishing Group

London Melbourne Sydney Auckland
Johannesburg and agencies throughout
the world

First published by Hutchinson 1984
Arrow edition 1985

Printed and bound in Great Britain by
Anchor Brendon Limited, Tiptree, Essex

ISBN 0 09 939630 0

For Robert

1

Big Sandy plunged his spade deep into the moist, black earth of his potato plot, holding it there lightly with one hand as he flexed his broad shoulders. Looking up, he scanned with narrowed eyes the distant outline of the road, so faintly etched against the rumpled hillside as to be barely identifiable save to the practised observer and then only by virtue of the telegraph poles which, like marker stakes against the vast background, irregularly picked out its route. After a few seconds he bent again to his task.

Several times during the past hour he had paused thus in a manner which, to an onlooker, would have suggested anticipation or even a degree of impatience. Yet, despite the seclusion of the croft and despite being unobserved except by Ben, his sheepdog, Sandy's habitually sphinx-like expression remained unchanged, revealing no trace of what thoughts might be passing through his mind.

Ben, nevertheless, had caught a suspicion of excitement. Lying at one end of the plot near Sandy's discarded jacket, he waited and watched, his body taut, ready for instant command; his vigilant eyes straying from his master's face only to flick a baleful glance at a lone gull which, gliding low overhead, broke the afternoon quiet with a few chattered comments before turning to swoop towards the shingle shore where the boundary of the croft met the restless jostlings of the sea.

Sandy had chosen this particular time of day to begin digging the ground ready for his potatoes because of the situation of the plot. From here, where he worked, he would be able to catch the first glimpse of the mail bus as it emerged from a narrow cleft in the hills to begin its meandering descent into the glen and round the shores of the loch. The moment the bus should come into view, Sandy had judged, would be the moment for him to abandon his digging for the day and return to the cottage. There he would blow up the smouldering peat fire into a cosy glow before hooking the kettle on its chain, all ready to welcome Mairi, his wife, who had been for two weeks in the city staying with her friend Buddy and was now coming home on the bus.

His watching was necessary since the bus ran to only a rough schedule, its primary function being not the carrying of passengers but the collection and transportation of mails to and from the mainland. There being much scope for contingencies at every stage of the journey, first by train, then by ferry and finally by bus, it was rarely possible to guess within an hour or so when it and its cargo of mails and passengers would eventually reach the village.

Sandy continued digging, steadily turning over the ground where, if the weather held, he and Mairi would soon be dibbling in their potatoes. The day was by no means warm; his movements were the easy practised ones of a man who has worked the land all his life but the weathered skin of his face glistened with sweat and there was a recurring dryness in his throat which had the effect of making him frequently want to swallow. With his foot poised on the spade, he turned and tried unsuccessfully to clear the dryness, at the same time taking the opportunity to make a more intense scrutiny of the road. Pushing back his cloth cap as if it interfered with his vision, he flung it so it landed on his jacket. Ben stood up, sniffed at the cap and then lay down again. Sandy wiped his sleeve over his brow and, rubbing his knuckles hard into the thatch of his black hair, allowed the cool breeze to freshen his scalp. Reflectively he assessed the area of turned earth before grasping his spade and resuming his digging.

He had completed the digging of two more furrows the full length of the plot before the bus came into view, crawling like a tiny explorative beetle along the intricacies of the road. As if reluctant to keep to his self-imposed plan, Sandy did not cease work immediately but turned over several more spadefuls of earth before finally wiping his spade on a tussock of sedge. Putting on his jacket, he made with purposeful strides towards the cottage.

The hens, clustered importunately around the door, scattered with wild shrieks and stray feathers as Ben, unbidden, chased them away. It was time for their evening feed but Sandy was indifferent to their pestering. Before she had gone away Mairi had pleaded, 'Unless the bus is fearfully late will you leave feeding the hens the evening I get back? He'll maybe like to help me to do that . . . and Sandy,' she had coaxed with a diffident smile, 'see there are a few eggs in the nestboxes for him to collect. Perhaps put some there if the hens haven't laid. Town children love to gather eggs.' Her lovely eyes had searched his face, anxious for his cooperation. Looking down at her, his grim expression had relaxed as his own eyes had humoured her with the tenderly indulgent smile only she ever saw.

When the peats were ablaze under the kettle he went over to the henhouse and with a slight sense of discomfiture checked that there were eggs in the nestboxes. Six altogether. That would be plenty, he told himself. Back at the cottage he poured rainwater into a bowl and washed his hands and face, afterwards tipping the water into a pail in which he dipped the stiff yardbrush and cleaned the worst of the mud from his boots. Finally he swept the kitchen floor. He was not a domesticated man. Indeed, Mairi would not have wished her man to be so, but he wanted to ensure that he had left no avoidable untidiness that might, even fractionally, mar the pleasure of her homecoming. For a few moments he surveyed the room and then, almost as if he had been denying the urge to do so, he went through into the narrow passageway which led to the back bedroom. Opening the door, he stood, letting his glance travel from the bed with its patchwork quilt made from knitted squares of wool that had come from their own sheep, to the curtains of homespun tweed which draped but did not screen the small window; from the shiny new linoleum which covered the floor to the low shelves beside the bed which Mairi had cajoled him into making and fixing. It was the first time he had seen the room all prepared and ready for occupancy and he found himself needing to take a deep slow breath as if to reassure himself. As he closed the door and the dryness again returned to his throat, he recognized and acknowledged the apprehension that had been dogging him for the past few months.

Going back into the kitchen and seeing the kettle already steaming, he swung it to one side and topped the glowing peats with still more peats to temporarily dampen down the flames. After a slight hesitation, as if secretly abashed at what he was about to do, he opened a drawer in the dresser and, taking out a blue and yellow patterned tablecloth, spread it over the shiny waxcloth which covered the bare wood of the table.

When they had first married Sandy had regarded with wry amusement Mairi's insistence on regularly covering the table with a cloth at mealtimes. In his own home even a covering of waxcloth had been regarded as a luxury. Admittedly his mother had possessed a tablecloth, but that had been of a sad brown colour which had been used only on Sabbath evenings when, with an air of reverence, it had been spread over the table, masking its workaday purpose and providing a more fitting resting place for the big Bible from which his father, until his death, and then his mother had read long passages aloud to the family. The ritual over, both cloth and Bible had been put away.

Such cloths as Mairi used would have been regarded as sinful frivolities by his parents' generation. Sandy himself recalled feeling slightly uneasy when Mairi had first produced one of her bright-coloured cloths, but he had understood that, having been used to being in service in big houses, Mairi naturally accepted the laying of a cloth as a prerequisite to any meal. He had doubted then that the habit would continue for long after she came to live on a croft that was without piped water and electricity and where ironing meant heating an old-fashioned box iron. The extra labour involved in laundering unnecessary tablecloths would, he reckoned, soon make her dispense with them. But he had been wrong. In the ten years they had been married not once had she set food before him without first covering the table with a prettily coloured cloth. She possessed a dozen or more of them, proudly bringing them back like trophies whenever she visited the mainland; even buying them from the heterogeneous bundles displayed by visiting tinkers. While she had been away Sandy had not thought to use a tablecloth, but now she was coming home he wanted the place to look as much like her home as he could and, as he smoothed down the cloth, he had to admit to himself that the kitchen was a livelier place for it, making the room look as if it too was eagerly awaiting the return of its mistress.

Had he not been a man, Sandy thought, he would have contemplated having ready for his wife the kind of repast she would have prepared for him had it been himself returning home after two weeks in the city. There would likely have been a chicken and vegetables in the pot, fresh bannocks and oatcakes kept warm by the hob, crowdie and butter, all of her own making; for though Mairi had come from the city she had soon adapted to being a crofter's wife and had become proud of her skills. She had filled the girnel before going to stay with her friend in the city but there was nothing home-baked in it now. Sandy did not reproach himself. In the Islands the demarcation line was strict. It was still 'man for the land and woman for the hearth'. The man of the house provided the food but it was the woman's task to prepare it and no one would have been more ashamed than Mairi had she allowed her man to turn his hand to the chores that were considered hers. Sandy had done as much as he could. The fish he had caught that day now lay filleted and sprinkled with salt on the slab in the larder. The potatoes were washed and ready for the pot. There were jugs of good fresh milk; there were eggs and there was still butter in the keg Mairi had salted down when there was a more than plenteous supply of cream. They would fare handsomely enough, thought Sandy, even without taking into account the extras Mairi would surely be bringing home from the mainland.

Pulling the door tight shut so as to prevent the hens from invading the kitchen while Ben was not there to harass them, Sandy strode easily, hands in pockets, along the narrow sheeptrack that wound between the rocky outcrops of the croft and led to the steps in the drystone wall near which the bus would deposit his wife. Just a few yards the croft side of the steps there was a high jutting slab of rock which in wild weather provided shelter for anyone, even a man of Sandy's height, while waiting for the bus. As the sound of the approaching bus grew louder a sudden impulse made Sandy seek the concealment of the rock and call Ben peremptorily to heel. He discovered he was sweating and was tempted to remove his jacket, but the cursed dryness was there again in his throat reminding him that it would very likely be futile to do so. His perspiration was not caused by the weather. Peering round the edge of the rock, Sandy watched the bus slow to a halt and as the door slid noisily back and his wife alighted he experienced the familiar leap of delight which the sight of her always brought him.

Ben rushed forward excitedly to greet Mairi, his barked welcome mixing with the called farewells of the passengers remaining on the bus. Sandy, on the point of emerging from his concealment as if he had in fact only that moment reached the spot, stood stock still. Dear God! No! No! The silent protest lodged in his chest and a gout of dismay rushed through him. As if stunned by a sudden blow, his eyes stayed fixed on the thin, frail-looking, be-spectacled young boy who, as soon as all Mairi's bags and parcels had been unloaded, had come half stumbling down the steps of the bus to stand, head hanging dejectedly, beside her. Surely not! Sandy's mind resisted the evidence of his eyes. There must have been some mistake, surely? Mairi would never have deceived him in this way; never have intended to lumber him with a burden such as this? The door of the bus slammed shut; the driver put the engine into gear. Sandy was swept by an overwhelming sense of betrayal. He felt a desire to stay hidden a little longer but already Mairi was looking around with puzzled expectancy, obviously wondering why he was not close behind Ben. With an air of complete composure he strode forward, remembering to salute the passengers on the departing bus as he did so, deliberately keeping his eyes averted from the unattractive child who stood beside his wife.

'Sandy!' She spoke his name joyously but the moment their eyes met he knew she had been expecting his disappointment and was now pleading mutely for his understanding. 'Dear,' she said, and as she drew the boy forward with a gentle hand on his arm, Sandy got the impression that she had rehearsed this meeting many times. 'Dear, this is Thomas. Thomas this is himself, my husband. I think you've been told a lot more about him than he's been told about you.'

'How do you do, Thomas.' Sandy did his best to infuse some warmth into his voice as he held out a steady hand. 'Welcome to Corrie.'

Mairi smiled at him gratefully but Thomas seemed uncertain for a moment whether or not he should make a reciprocal gesture. When his small pale hand did touch Sandy's he withdrew it instantly as if pricked by a thistle. Furtively he glanced up and immediately looked down again, either too shy or too miserable to venture a smile or a word. Mairi, aware of the bleakness of Sandy's expression, said hurriedly, 'Oh, but we've had such a journey with one thing and then another. We'll both be glad to get a nice cup of tea inside us, is that not so, Thomas?'

Sandy thought he detected the boy's head move slightly in response to her words. 'Right then,' he said. 'Let's get you back to the cottage.' He picked up the two suitcases. 'Leave the rest of your parcels and I'll come back for them later on.' His voice was terse, making plain his impatience to get moving.

'Oh, no,' Mairi insisted. 'The rest of the bags aren't heavy at all and Thomas and I are quite strong enough to carry them ourselves, aren't we, Thomas?' She smiled encouragingly at the boy. 'But first Thomas must say a proper how do you do to Ben.' She called to Ben, who had already started to follow his master but who, at her summons, bounded back happily to be fussed over. 'You and Ben will soon be good friends, I'm sure,' Mairi said.

Glancing back, Sandy saw Thomas's stiff reaction to Ben's vigorous welcome. His mouth twitched cynically. The boy looks as if he'd be scared of a wee spider never mind a great lump of a sheepdog, he thought.

Arriving first at the cottage, Sandy took the larger of the two suitcases into his and Mairi's bedroom where he left it on the bed ready for her to unpack. The smaller one he placed on the bed in the back room.

'There now!' Mairi smiled warmly at her husband as she came into the kitchen. 'Just look at that, Thomas! A lovely fire and a singing kettle to welcome us home. Is that not good to see?' So far as Sandy could make out she was still getting no perceptible response from the boy but undeterred she went on, 'I will take off my hat and coat now and put on my gumboots. You come through into your bedroom and do the same. And put on that jacket

you got from Andy. We must hurry if we're going to feed
the hens before they get tired of waiting and go off to their
roosts for the night without any supper. And we'll look to
see if they've laid any eggs for our breakfast in the morning, like I promised you.' She turned to dart a question-
ingly conspiratorial glance at Sandy before taking
Thomas off to his bedroom. When she returned she was
carrying the small suitcase. 'Oh, Sandy,' she called as he
was about to go outside, 'it's the big suitcase that is to go
into Thomas's room. This small one has my own things in
it.'

Sandy took the larger suitcase through to the back room
where Thomas was standing looking out of the window.
'That's yours, I believe,' he said. 'Will I put it on the bed?'

Thomas nodded spectrally.

'He seems to be well provided for if he's needing a
suitcase that heavy for his things,' Sandy observed to
Mairi as he closed the door of the passageway behind him.

'That's because he's had so many things given to him,'
she explained. Seeing his brows lift uncomprehendingly,
she went on, 'While I was telling Buddy I would need to
get Thomas some good weatherproof clothes, seeing he'd
only thin ones suited to city life, Buddy's neighbour came
in. A few minutes after she'd gone she was back again with
a big parcel of clothes her own son had grown out of. Good
ones they were too, and she was so pleased at being able to
pass them on to someone she knew, I hadn't the heart to
refuse them.' She caught her husband's glance of
annoyance. 'I insisted on giving her something for them,
of course,' she placated him, 'but it was nothing like they
would have cost new.'

Sandy seemed unappeased. 'Surely, Mairi, you knew I
would not have begrudged having to spend on new clothes
for the boy,' he reproved her. His pride was hurt.
Although he had not her interest in the boy he was willing

16

to accept it as his duty to provide for him as lavishly as she thought needful.

She came and leaned against him and as her hand went up to caress his cheek his arms closed round her. 'Dear,' she explained, 'it's not just as simple as that. When you've been in an orphanage you kind of get used to hand-me-downs. You long for new clothes, of course, but I can still remember how strange it felt when I was given a complete brand new outfit to wear. The prospect was exciting and I felt as proud as a peacock, and yet there was this strangeness because not one of the things I was wearing had belonged to any of the bigger girls before me. They hadn't the right feel to them somehow. I suppose it's a little like getting into a bed and lying beside someone who's already taken the chill off it, rather than getting into a cold empty one and warming it yourself.' Her lips curved in a small, nostalgic smile. 'The strangeness didn't last long because I was staying on at the orphanage then, but remembering it made me realize that leaving the orphanage and coming to live here with us is such a tremendously new experience for Thomas. To be dressed in all new clothes, I thought, might accentuate the feeling of unfamiliarity.' She shrugged, keeping her shoulders lifted as she went on. 'It's not easy to explain but I feel strongly that we must try not to thrust too many new experiences on him too suddenly. I think he should be gentled into his new life.' She waited, looking up at him as if wanting his approval. 'You see, he'd already met Andy and obviously he admired him a lot so I think he was quite thrilled to be presented with the clothes Andy had grown out of. Maybe he thought they'd help him to grow more like Andy.'

Sandy nodded slowly, accepting her reasoning though only half appreciating it. As so often happened, he felt humbled by her perception and understanding. Swiftly he lifted her until her face was level with his. 'Glad to have me back again are you?' she murmured, her cheek against his.

'Would you believe me if I said I wasn't,' he teased, his hard mouth softening as it moved over her fair hair. Abruptly he set her down. 'Go and feed your hens, woman,' he bade her, though his strong hands made no effort to relax their grip on her shoulders. His eyes dwelt on the sweet curve of her lips as she smiled at him provocatively. He knew himself to be a stern man – stern even with his own emotions – but this small shining woman he held imprisoned in his grasp could so easily shatter his composure. His voice rasped in his throat. 'Go now, while I can still let you go,' he told her.

Laughingly she broke away from him. 'Aye, and if you don't get out and see to your sheep, you'll need to be chasing them with a lamp,' she warned him.

He lifted the smaller suitcase from the table where she had put it and took it through to their bedroom. As he stood recovering from the effect of her nearness he heard her calling Thomas. Returning to the kitchen, he was in time to see them both go past the window on their way to feed the hens.

2

At the edge of the moor where the land began to rear steeply to merge with the hills, Sandy leaned on his crook, watching his flock of sheep, many of them still heavy in lamb, grazing their leisurely way towards the sheltered corrie where they would spend the night. Ben stood beside him, quiveringly eager for the command to herd them. But the command did not come. The sheep were moving placidly, not bunching together as they would if there was a suspicion of danger and Sandy, seeing no reason to harry them unnecessarily, spoke a monosyllabic veto to Ben and turned back in the direction of his croft. Almost argumentatively Ben stood for a moment looking from his master to the sheep before giving in and following to heel.

The gathering dusk was being thickened now by a thin drizzle of chill rain and as Sandy retraced his path he could see two faint glimmers of lamplight from the windows of the cottage. He was used to seeing only the lighted window of the kitchen at this hour, but he remembered that Mairi would no doubt be in their bedroom taking the opportunity to unpack her suitcase and put away her city clothes.

By the time he reached the cobbled path that led to the door of the house the drizzle had developed into a heavy downpour. Ben, preceding him now in his anxiety for the meal that would be awaiting him, became suddenly alert and then, to Sandy's surprise, made as if to go round to the back of the house. Sandy, suspecting the dog had picked up the track of some predator intent on pillaging Mairi's henhouse, made to follow, but at the corner of the house Ben halted and began whining a greeting.

The dark figure which stood close against the wall of the house bent forward to pat Ben briefly before retreating again into the shadows. All Sandy could be sure he was seeing was a pale face uplifted to the rain. Thomas! Astonished, Sandy almost spoke the name aloud. What was the boy doing standing out there in the darkness and getting soaked by the chill rain? Had Thomas been a crofter child he would have thought nothing of his being there since crofter children seemed from birth to be weather-resistant. But this delicate city child? He wondered at Mairi allowing him to be out there; wondered if indeed she knew he was there; wondered why the boy was standing so strangely still; and then, with a stab of compunction, he wondered if Thomas's face was uplifted to the rain so it might wash away the evidence of tears. Momentarily nonplussed as to how he should react, Sandy limited himself to calling a banal comment on the weather. There was no audible reply and with a sense of having been rebuffed Sandy turned and went into the cottage.

In the kitchen Mairi was humming to herself as she lifted fresh-baked scones from the girdle and wrapped them in a clean teatowel.

'The rain is on again,' he remarked, thinking that if she knew Thomas was out there she would immediately call him inside.

'Indeed I saw that,' she replied. 'Weren't we lucky it waited until we got home?' Sandy shot her a veiled glance but her attention was on her baking. She made no allusion to Thomas.

Pulling a sack from the pile behind the door, Sandy rubbed the worst of the wet from Ben's shaggy coat before he himself sat down and pulled off his boots. 'You've gotten yourself busy already,' he observed to Mairi. 'I was thinking you would be after bringing back fancy breads from the city for us to eat tonight.'

'And so I did.' Mairi flashed him a warm, teasing smile. 'But tell me now, who would be content to eat city food when he could be eating fresh scones from the girdle? Not you, Sandy MacDonald. Not you, indeed.'

The creases at the corners of Sandy's eyes deepened in acknowledgement of her banter. 'I would have eaten it though and saved you having to start baking the minute you got indoors,' he rejoined.

'Ach, it's just that I cannot help spoiling you, fool that I am,' she returned lightly. Her voice grew soft. 'It's what I miss doing when I'm away from you, so I'm glad to be starting again.' She was brushing the flour from the girdle into the fire and her back was towards him, so she missed seeing the depth of tenderness in the look he gave her. But she knew instinctively that it would be there; guessed that he would be covertly watching her as she put away the girdle and spread yet another bright new cloth on the table. She herself was wearing an apron which she had also brought back from the city. Darting a quick, mischievous look at him she caught him unawares as he watched her.

'How do you like my new apron?' she asked, smiling archly at him as she saw the faint flush that always touched his cheekbones when he was embarrassed.

'I was thinking what a swank you're looking tonight,' he said as he bent to put on the slippers she had placed in readiness under his chair. There was a flurry of rain against the window and the catch of the outer door rattled. Mairi glanced at the door.

'The wind's getting up again,' she commented.

'Aye.' Reaching out an arm, Sandy picked up the newspaper she had brought for him. 'I take it you know the boy is out there in the rain?' he said with forced nonchalance.

'I do indeed.' Mairi sounded a trifle piqued by his question. 'Did you think I wouldn't be knowing where he is and him only a couple of hours hardly in the house?'

'I was surprised to see him,' he admitted. 'It's pretty wet out there and he looks kind of frail to be getting a drenching. It's not a thing he can be used to, I reckon.'

Mairi moved over to sit on his knee. 'That's just it,' she told him. 'He's certainly not used to it. Someone would have got into trouble for allowing him to do it. I'm thinking maybe he's out there because that's one of the things he's always wanted to do.' Sandy cocked an eyebrow. 'Yes,' she went on, 'just that. To stand out in the rain and let it soak through his clothes. I'm not going to call him in. Not for a whiley, anyway.' Sandy rested an arm lightly around her as she made herself more comfortable on his lap. 'You know, kids do have secret longings to do what seem to adults to be the silliest and simplest things.' She sighed reflectively. 'We used to confess our secret longings to one another sometimes after lights out at night. You know, the sort of things we'd seen or read about other children doing but which we never seemed to get the chance to do because we were in a home. I remember one girl saying the thing she most wanted to do was to walk with one foot on the pavement and one in the gutter so that she bobbed along as if she had a peg leg. We all thought that was terribly funny. Another wanted to sit on a kitchen table and swing her legs while she stuffed cakes fresh from the oven. That was her idea of having a real home. Yet another longed to swing on an iron gate, letting it clang shut again and again.' Mairi gazed up at the ceiling as if abstracting memories from the air. 'They were such trivial things, mostly. Little mind pictures that we yearned to make come true just once in a while.' She shrugged. 'But we were too well disciplined.' She felt Sandy's arm tighten around her. 'Not cruelly so, of course, but enough to have to subdue our little yearnings.'

'And what was your own secret longing?' Sandy asked.

'Oh, I was so greedy. I had lots, but the one I best remember is wanting to put orange peel in a puddle and then tread it down with my boot heel so the oil squeezed out and made little swirlies of colour which floated on the water. I'd seen a girl do it once, but I wasn't allowed to get my boots wet.' She smiled reminiscently. 'The first chance I got I did it, but it was a fearful disappointment. Perhaps I'd got too old by then to enjoy it the same.' She chuckled. 'Or perhaps it was the orange that was too old because there seemed to be no oil in the skin to squeeze out.'

She sprang up from his knee at the sound of the door opening. Thomas came in. His hair was plastered down with rain and he was having to screw up his eyes against the light, but he looked strangely elated.

'Goodness me, Thomas, but how wet you are. Give me your jacket to dry it and then you go through to your bedroom and change into dry clothes.' The trace of scolding in her voice was deliberate, Sandy suspected, more to reassure the boy than to scold him. He watched obliquely as Thomas took his spectacles out of his jacket pocket and laid them on the table. 'They'll be all misted up with the rain,' Mairi said, picking up the spectacles and polishing them on her apron. Thomas peered at her shortsightedly as she handed them back to him. 'Now away to your room and get into some dry clothes. And be quick because your food will be waiting for you. I'm ready for putting it out right now, so see you don't leave it till it gets cold.' Thomas scurried away obediently.

Sandy pulled a chair up to the table and sat waiting. 'The boy looks as if he's needing a good feeding,' he commented as Mairi ladled fish and potatoes onto his plate. 'I reckon they don't get overfed in these homes.'

'Oh, that's not true,' Mairi denied. 'Not these days. There was always plenty at our orphanage and I dare say that's true of the rest. But it's institution food. Sometimes we liked it, sometimes we didn't. Never anything different to look forward to, though. You know what I mean. But then, I suppose,' she added thoughtfully, 'it must be difficult to please so many children and it stands to reason they couldn't encourage faddiness. If you didn't like what was there you just had to go without or fill up with bread and what passed for butter. There was always plenty of that.'

'And will you be encouraging faddiness?' Sandy asked.

She put food on Thomas's plate and on her own plate

and sat down at the table before replying. Aware that Sandy was still regarding her quizzically, she rested her chin on her hands. 'I might, just to begin with,' she conceded.

'Is it not best to start the way you mean to go on?' he cautioned. 'It will likely be easier for you in the long run.'

'There's not such a lot of variety for him to be choosy about, is there?' she riposted.

Thomas came into the kitchen. He had changed into dry clothes and had rubbed his hair into tousled dryness.

'There now,' Mairi smiled at him. 'Come and sit you down and himself will say Grace.' They bowed their heads.

Later in the evening, when a tired Thomas had taken his candle and gone to bed, there was an unusually long silence between Mairi and Sandy.

'Well,' Mairi said at last with a note of challenge in her voice, 'what have you to say to me, Sandy MacDonald?' She had taken up her knitting and Sandy, having filled and lit the one pipeful of tobacco he allowed himself of an evening, had settled himself in his chair with the newspaper, his long legs stretched towards the hearth.

'I was thinking of asking you if you'd enjoyed your stay with Buddy and Dr Nigel,' he replied.

'Indeed I did so,' she told him. 'And both of them were on at me again to persuade you to leave this backwards place and go to live near them. We'd be able to have a nice house with electricity and a bathroom and the shops handy. Nigel has a busy practice and he's on several committees so he has plenty of influence. He reckons he could arrange for a good job to be waiting for you to step into.' She avoided looking at him while she was speaking.

'Is that so?' Sandy's voice and attitude were expressive of the total disinterest of a man accustomed to being teased on the subject. He continued reading his paper and while she studied his profile Mairi's lips tilted in a fond smile. She had been teasing him, of course. She invariably teased him so when she returned from the city, passing on, in some measure, the teasing she got from friends about burying herself in the country. There were times when she allowed herself to ponder over whether, were she seriously to demand it of him, his devotion to her would lead him to renounce this place and the life he loved to become a city dweller, no matter how repellent the prospect. She suspected he might be prepared to make even that sacrifice. But she knew, beyond all doubt, that she would never ask it of him. Though she herself had grown up against a city background, she had become more than content with the crofting life she shared with him. She enjoyed a visit to the city on occasion – even indulged herself by envying the relative ease of the city housewife's life – but so completely had she succumbed to the beauty of the island with its gaunt hills and wide skies, its seascapes and sunsets, its patchwork of crofts, its clean, so clean rain and soft mists through which rainbows frequently danced and shimmered against the mosaic of the moors, that she could recall no single moment of nostalgia for the city. Despite the toil entailed by lack of amenities, she knew, and she guessed her husband also knew, that should he ever propose their moving to the city it would be she herself who would resist.

The wall clock ticked on hollowly; Ben snored behind Sandy's chair; the rain driven by the rapidly rising wind spattered like hail against the window. Sandy, aware that Mairi was directing anxious glances towards him, waited for her to speak. When she did she put to him the question he had been dreading.

'You aren't very pleased with me for bringing Thomas here, are you, Sandy?'

'I agreed to it,' he countered flatly.

'Yes, I know you did. But you hadn't seen him then. Now that you have seen him you're disappointed, aren't you?' Her troubled eyes were wide above the spectacles she wore perched on the end of her nose whenever she was knitting some intricate pattern. She saw her husband's jaw tighten for an instant before he replied.

'I'll not deny I'd expected you'd choose a boy that had the making of a man in him. Someone that looked stronger and healthier altogether. I'll feel ashamed. . . .' He stopped short, realizing how much his words were upsetting her.

'You were expecting someone bonnier altogether,' she pressed him.

'What man wouldn't?' Her hurt expression stung him but he could not hide the truth of what he felt. His voice became resentful. 'I cannot understand why you'd choose such a shrimp of a lad, Mairi.' He nodded towards the door that led to Thomas's bedroom. 'He looks as if the first gale of wind will wither him.' Half turning towards her, he saw the tenseness of her attitude. Uneasily he went on, 'He's not right for either of us, Mairi. You'll soon see the life here will be too tough for him and then what will happen? He'll be wanting back to where he came from and your heart will be full of new grief.' He paused and after he had cleared his throat his voice became gentler. 'It's you I'm thinking of, Mairi.'

Mairi's hands rested on the knitting in her lap. 'Dear, he won't want back,' she said confidently. 'Not if we can give him a loving home. Nothing else will matter.' Her voice was full of appeal. 'And though he looks frail enough now, what better place than this can there be for helping him grow big and strong? Only try to make him welcome, dear. Please do try, for my sake.'

The tears glistening in her eyes discomfited Sandy.

'You know I will. You know fine I'll do just that, seeing you're so keen to have him here,' he confirmed emphatically. 'But he's not helping me much when all I've got when I've spoken to him is a bare nod. I've not heard the poor creature speak a single word either to you or myself since he got here,' he defended himself indignantly.

'Yes, dear, I know. But it's so difficult for him,' Mairi explained. 'You see, dear, he stammers very badly and it gets much worse when he's nervous, which he naturally would be meeting you for the first time.' There was an anxious frown on her brow. 'He's not backward,' she was quick to assure him. 'He knows what he wants to say but when he tries to speak, the words just won't come. It makes him so ashamed he just hangs his head and tries not to look at anyone.'

Oh, God! No! Sandy felt a new sense of outrage. A nervous, sickly looking creature with bad eyesight was surely burden enough for them to take on, but now, to learn that a bad stammer was yet another of his handicaps! What next would he discover? He stared morosely into the fire, fearing to look in his wife's direction lest his expression should betray the depth of his disillusionment.

'He'll get better, I'm sure,' Mairi was saying. 'But you see, dear, you're very big and strong and you have such a grim expression always that you can be quite frightening to anyone who doesn't know you. Especially to a youngster. Once he gets used to you, I'm certain you'll get on just fine together. Be patient, dear. I do so want the three of us to be happy.' Sandy gave a resigned nod.

After a few minutes of silence Mairi yawned and, putting down her knitting, got up from her chair. 'There's such a lot I have to put to rights before I can go to my bed,' she said and went through to the bedroom where he heard her opening and closing drawers.

Contrary to his usual habit, Sandy relit his pipe and settled back in his chair. He still held the newspaper in front of him but his mind was ranging back over the years since he had met and married Mairi, recalling the sequence of events which had begun three years ago and which had now led to the presence of Thomas in their home.

3

Three times in the first five years of their marriage Mairi had become pregnant, yet she had never succeeded in bearing a child. She had so much wanted a family that it had come as a crushing blow when, her third miscarriage having put her own life at risk, the doctors had made it impossible for her to conceive again.

She had struggled hard not to inflict her grief on Sandy,

but he, knowing how much she had yearned for a child and with what joy she had spoken of the prospect, felt stricken whenever he saw the secret anguish which showed in her hollowed, dark-shadowed eyes. There were times when her suffering made him feel traitorous, his own sorrow being relatively shallow when contrasted with his unbounding relief that Mairi had been spared to him. There were times when he felt shamed by the inadequacy of his efforts to comfort her.

It was not only the loss of the babies that had kept her spirits low. 'Folks in these parts think little of a woman who cannot bear her man a child,' she had sobbed. And he, all too aware of the truth of her assertion, could only offer the solace of a dismissive epithet on their stupidity.

But with time Mairi had recovered well enough to conceal all signs that she might be grieving still over her childlessness. And then about three years ago the postman had brought her a letter which, though neither she nor Sandy could have known it at the time, was radically to affect their lives.

The letter was from a girl with whom Mairi had been friendly when they had been children together at the orphanage. 'She'd been christened Rosebud,' Mairi had told him, her voice teetering on a giggle. 'That's the name she was known by at the home and she hated it. She used to shrivel every time she heard it.' Mairi's giggle broke into a laugh. 'She always said she knew perfectly well she never had and never would look like a rosebud. More like a warty carrot, she used to say, because her hair was red. Actually I remember her as being quite attractive. Just a bit big for her age and a bit bumpy in shape, and she used to get pimples on her face quite a lot,' Mairi reminisced. 'I nicknamed her Buddy and she liked that much better. We soon found we laughed at the same things and dreamed much the same dreams, so in spite of the difference in size

– I was a shrimp then – we got on well together. I missed her a lot when the time came for her to leave.' A small frown appeared between Mairi's eyes as if she was having difficulty in remembering. 'She left about six months before I did and she took up nursing. I had one letter from her telling me she was enjoying her job and I replied telling her I was going into service. It was years before I heard from her again and that letter came from Canada where she'd taken a temporary job. By that time I was working here at the Laird's house.' She looked at Sandy and her face creased into a roguish smile. 'D'you know, I distinctly remember writing and telling her about the big handsome man who used to bring lobsters for the Laird. I said all the maids were in love with him but that I found him a bit scary and had christened him The Sphinx because no one ever saw him smile. I wonder if she'll remember my telling her that?' Her laughter pealed out. 'What fun it's going to be to write and tell her I married my Sphinx.'

Buddy had written to say she was now married to a doctor and was living in the city; that they had two children; that if her letter ever reached Mairi, she would very much like her to get in touch and perhaps pay them a visit if she felt so inclined.

'Oh, I'd dearly love to see her again,' Mairi had cried enthusiastically, and Sandy, always anxious for her happiness, had given his encouragement. Mairi's stay had lasted three weeks. She had come back much refreshed and with an invitation from Buddy and her husband to visit them again the following year. It had been subsequent to this second visit that Mairi had put to him the suggestion that they might consider fostering a child. 'Not a wee bairn,' she had hastened to stress. 'I reckon I'd be considered too old for that now – but perhaps one of school age or thereabouts.'

Her suggestion had so thrown Sandy that his impassivity had given way to a moment of sharp surprise. Mairi's clear grey eyes had regarded him steadily. 'The ache hasn't gone altogether,' she had explained simply.

'No!' His tone was stilted, as if the word had been wrung out of him. Objections chased one another through his mind but he baulked at voicing them.

'Why so, all of a sudden?' he found himself saying.

'Oh, it's not sudden at all, dear,' she had surprised him by saying. 'It's an idea that's been plaguing the back of my mind for a whiley now. I don't know . . . perhaps ever since . . . ' She broke off, shaking her head as if confused by her own thoughts. 'I didn't speak of it to you because I kept telling myself I wasn't being fair to you even thinking of it.'

'Mairi!' There was reproof in his voice.

'Oh, Sandy! But a man wants his own. Any woman knows that.' She was standing by the table and he saw her fingers clench and unclench as she held the edge of it. 'I cannot give you your own, that's why I felt it wasn't fair. But then, the first time I went to stay with Buddy, she took me with her on a visit to the local orphanage – or children's home as they're known nowadays. Being a nurse and a doctor's wife as well as having been reared in an orphanage, she feels well qualified to keep an eye on things so she visits regularly. I went several times while I was there. It was a happy enough place but we both remembered the little things that don't show no matter how much they hurt: the emptiness one felt when one of the children went for adoption and you wondered why they'd been chosen and not you. That in itself made you feel unattractive. Then there was the criticism if you were a bit rebellious sometimes or if you were slow in being grateful even for something you didn't want or particularly like. Kids can be damned unhappy without showing it.' Her eyes had grown shadowed with remembered sadness and it was several seconds before she spoke again. 'Buddy and Nigel have adopted two children since my first visit,' she said, 'a boy and a girl about the same ages as her own two and they're settled as though they've always belonged there.' Her eyes glowed softly as though she was seeing the four children playing together. 'I'd kind of like to do that for a child,' she said.

To Sandy's relief she had not pursued the subject at the time but, as he knew she would, she had touched on the subject at intervals, not pressing him for a decision but leaving him in no doubt that she was not going to give up the idea easily. He had proffered reasons against her proposal. Might not the taking of a child into their home reawaken past grief? Might it not disrupt their life together, bringing regret rather than happiness? It was not unknown for such things to happen. She had listened to him gravely, her own reasoning blunting his objections. He was still loath to take a strange child into his home, but he knew, despite all his misgivings, he would yield to her entreaties. She had always given him so much and asked so little in return, he could refuse her nothing that would add to her happiness. If fostering a child would help assuage the ache that lingered in her heart, he must be willing not only to accept his share of the responsibility but also to try to warm to the prospect.

'There's so much love we have here in this cottage, dear,' she had whispered when she was finally assured of his acquiescence. 'There's surely some we could spare for a child who has maybe never had very much.' She had been standing behind his chair then, her arms warm around his neck and, inclining his head, he had rubbed his chin against the smooth skin of her hand. 'Buddy wants me to go and stay again before the end of next month because they're all going off to the States for a whole year.

Nigel is going to do some research there, it seems. That means I shan't see them until the following year if I don't go soon.'

'So?' His tone had been one of lenient surprise.

'Well, if you agree, I'd like to bring a child back with me. It would be only on a trial basis to see if he likes it here. We'd have to get all sorts of papers signed before we could officially adopt him.'

She felt him stiffen slightly. 'Him? You already have a child in mind, then?'

'Yes,' she acknowledged. He had noticed the slight catch in her breath. 'His name is Thomas and he's eight years old.'

'Next month seems kind of soon,' Sandy prevaricated.

'Towards the end of next month,' she had pointed out. 'Nigel will arrange it all, seeing he's on the committee and seeing it was he who put forward the idea in the first place.' She paused. 'The doctor here and the nurse and the minister will vouch for you if it's needed, surely.' She paused again. 'I really would like to bring him then.'

'Why not?' The disquiet he felt at the imminent sharing of his home had not been detectable in his voice.

'Dear!' Coming round to the front of his chair, Mairi had dropped a soothing kiss on his brow.

She had been happily painting in the spare bedroom one day in preparation for the new arrival when Sandy had come in. 'My, but that looks fine,' he had observed. 'He'll be greatly taken with all you're doing for him, I'm thinking.'

'I hope he will be.' She had not looked up from her painting. 'You haven't asked me much about Thomas, have you?' she had reproached him. 'Aren't you at all curious to know if he has dark or fair hair; whether it's curly or straight; whether he's short and chubby or whether he's tall for his age? If it had been you who had done the choosing, I would have been bursting with questions as to what he looked like.'

'That's because you're a woman,' he had parried. 'Anyway, have I not always trusted your judgement?'

All he had known about Thomas at that stage was that his mother had died while he was still an infant; that he had then been looked after by his granny until her death when he was only five years old; and that since then he had been cared for at the orphanage where Mairi had found him. For Sandy that much knowledge had sufficed. His mind had shaped no image of the boy they might expect. Boys were boys; some quiet; some mischievous; some wily. Mairi would have chosen well, he had no doubt, nor had he any doubt that in time they would all grow accustomed to one another. He had seen no reason for probing further.

Moving furniture into the back bedroom in readiness, laying new linoleum and constructing shelves had succeeded, as Mairi had hoped, in tempering Sandy's misgivings with interest. There had even been moments – though quickly banished – when he had suspected himself of actually looking forward to having a youngster about the place. A boy he might teach to row and to fish; to set creels; in time to involve himself with the work of the croft. But his first meeting with Thomas had instantly dispelled the interest that had begun to flicker within him. He knew that for Mairi's sake he must make allowances for the boy; that he must fight his disappointment and try his best to take to him. But in his own mind he knew that even if Thomas should want to settle permanently with Mairi and himself, he would never measure up to his own idea of what a boy should be.

He was staring morosely into the fire when Mairi came back into the kitchen. He noticed she was carrying her nightdress over her arm. As she draped it over a stool to warm in front of the fire Sandy raised a quizzical brow. It was unusual for her to warm her nightdress except in the coldest of weather. 'I'm feeling the cold something terrible tonight,' she told him with a little shiver.

Sandy, his own body almost feverish with desire for her, spoke with concern. 'I hope that doesn't mean you've caught a chill?'

'No, I think I just got a wee bit cold on the ferry coming over,' she yawned.

He gave her a meaningful glance. 'You'll soon be warm enough,' he told her.

She smiled vaguely and went back into the bedroom from whence she returned carrying a small flat box. 'You'll be wanting to see the birthday present you're to give me,' she said, handing it to him.

Birthdays went unobserved in crofting communities, and Mairi's insistence on presents whenever either of their birthdays came round was yet another of the innovations Sandy had come to accept. But since he left the island rarely, and then only to attend cattle or sheep sales which were held well on the outskirts of even the smallest towns, he had to give Mairi the money to buy whatever she fancied as her present from him. Opening the box, he saw it contained an arrangement of embroidered handkerchieves. 'Nice,' he commented, giving the box back to her. It pleased him more and more to know that she liked pretty things.

'They're special,' she said, and added with a chuckle, 'The Dear knows if I shall ever get round to wiping my nose on one.'

She went into the larder and returned carrying a pan half full of milk which she set on the hob beside the fire. From the dresser cupboard she took out a glass and a bottle of whisky which she set on the table within Sandy's reach. When the milk was hot she filled a mug and sat sleepily sipping while her husband, after knocking out his pipe, poured whisky into his glass.

Mairi yawned again. 'Indeed, I'm as tired as an old dog,' she said. 'I can never remember being as tired as I am this night.' She finished her milk and picked up her nightie, hugging its warmth against her bosom. 'I'll not wait for you tonight, dear,' she said.

Sandy drained his glass. 'I'm coming too,' he said, getting up and preparing to extinguish the lamp.

'Sandy, please,' she whispered, putting out a hand as if to restrain him. 'I'm so very tired. Tomorrow night . . . ? Please?' she entreated.

She saw the swift look of chagrin and disappointment that crossed his face as he stared at her. His lips tightened and, turning from her, he poured himself more whisky, tossing it back as if it had been a mere sip.

'If that's the way you want it,' he said resignedly.

Instead of following her through to the bedroom he opened the door of the cottage and stood for some minutes peering out into the wind-hustled darkness. Already, so it seemed to him, the presence of the boy Thomas had begun to come between him and Mairi.

4

Thomas woke early, screwing up his eyes against a shaft of steel-bright sunshine which had been newly released from a canopy of morning mist. Drawing up the sheet so as to shut out the brightness, he lay for some minutes wondering a little nervously what he could expect to happen on this first day of his new life. When he had been shown his bedroom the previous evening, his apprehension had been much relieved by its smallness. When he had come to bed, the golden glow of candlelight coupled with the curiously friendly smell of melting wax had helped chase away the last straggling fears of the unknown. When he had got into bed and pulled up the bedclothes, the scent of bog myrtle, which Mairi always used among her stored bedding, had struck him as oddly pleasing, so different from the nondescript smell of his bed at the orphanage that he had soon breathed himself into smiling drowsiness. When Mairi had looked in to dout the candle, he had been fast asleep.

The shaft of sunlight faded and Thomas sat up, appreciating the slowly mounting thrill of finding himself alone. Swinging his legs from under the bedclothes, he let his feet snug into the curly sheepskin as he sat on the edge of the bed, savouring the knowledge that this was the first morning he could recall being wakened by the sun shining on him from between undrawn curtains. At the orphanage it had always been noises which had awakened him: doors slamming; footsteps thumping on the stairs and along the corridors; voices, sometimes querulous, sometimes demanding; bells. As he surveyed his room, he was again conscious of how differently it smelled from the rooms and corridors of the Home. Deciding that he liked it, he told himself it must be the smell of cosiness as opposed to emptiness. He swung his legs back onto the bed and sat cuddling his knees. This was his own room! His and no one else's. Mrs Mairi, as he still called her, had promised him that, and he knew that, more than anything else, he wanted to believe she would keep any promise she made him. Cautiously he tried bouncing on the bed. It creaked a little but it seemed to Thomas that they were creaks of acceptance rather than protest.

He pulled the clothes round him again, reminding himself Mrs Mairi had told him he needn't get up until he

wanted to. Not until he started school. His spirits plum-
meted momentarily at the thought of school, but he
pushed it to the back of his mind. Discovering he was
eager to get up, he pushed back the bedclothes and slid his
feet into the slippers which had been placed handily
beside the bed. 'I will have no bare feet in my dormitory,'
the remembered voice of authority assailed him as he
looked down at his feet. The slippers were orphanage
slippers and smacked of orders. Defiantly Thomas kicked
them off and padded barefoot over the linoleum to stand
in front of the window.

The cottage was of the type usually described as a 'but
and ben': squat and single-storeyed and comprising only a
kitchen and a bedroom, between which there was a small
hallway where gumboots and oilskins could be left to dry.
Soon after Sandy and Mairi had married they had, in
expectation of the family they planned, built onto the back
of the house to provide a small extra bedroom and also a
pantry, the two divided by a passageway which led from
the kitchen. The windows of the two front rooms of the
house gave a wide view of the croft and beyond that of the
sea, but the back bedroom which was now Thomas's
looked out onto an area of spare grass and dark, almost
black, earth, pitted with the hoof marks of cattle and now,
after the rain of the previous night, shining moistly in the
patchy morning sunlight. The area was bounded by a low,
drystone wall within which stood the cow byre, a window-
less drystone building, roofed with black felt and breached
by a single door, near which there reposed a sizeable dung
heap. Sheltered by the nearer gable of the byre stood a
couple of dumpy haystacks weighted down by boulders
and covered with tarpaulins. Beyond the boundary wall
Thomas could see that the land rose steeply as the rough
grass gave way to heather clumps, the heather to crags of
grey rock which looked as if they had long ago rolled there

after breaking away from the distant hills, the shapes of which were still obscured by the swirling mist.

What would have seemed to many to be a cheerless view did not disappoint Thomas. 'Wildness and wet you must expect, Thomas,' Mairi had stressed, not wanting him to have any illusions about the place he was coming to. Wildness and wet there was indeed, Thomas thought, but was it not proof that he could rely on Mrs Mairi to tell him the truth? There would be howling gales to contend with too, she had told him. Gales that could blow a man's feet from under him and drive the rain so hard you felt as if you were being hit by pellets from a gun. 'But on calm days,' Thomas remembered how her voice had deepened with enthusiasm as she spoke . . . 'on calm days there are wide, wide skies such as you've never before thought possible anywhere in the world. And the clouds can smile as well as weep; the sea can whisper as well as roar. And you will see rainbows, Thomas. Such rainbows! Until you've seen a Corrie rainbow, you haven't seen one that's worth a second look. So many there are, I think sometimes how deserted the sky can look when it's not tied with a rainbow.'

Standing there by the window, Thomas caught his breath incredulously. Even as he watched, a rainbow began to emerge from the mist, reticently at first and then more decisively, until it had formed an arc of such vividness that its shimmering splendour appeared to imprint a secondary arc, only a fraction less brilliant, on the sombre slopes of the hills. Thomas, enraptured by the sight, could hardly breathe. He could see one end of the rainbow and, pressing his face against the windowpane, he strained to see if he could see the other end, but the window was too small. Although he had seen rainbows before, they had been rare sights and pallid in contrast. Never had he seen or dreamed of seeing a rainbow which seemed to dominate

the sky with its brilliance and looked sturdy enough for
him to climb, had he really wanted to. He ran quickly to
the door of his room, intent on dashing outside to try and
chase the rainbow, but remembering he was not dressed,
not even wearing the hitherto compulsory slippers, he
shuffled his feet into them. He knew he ought to dress but
there was no time and Mrs Mairi would surely understand the urgency, he told himself. She would be eager for
him to see such a sight. But as his hand grasped the latch
his resolve faltered. Supposing he should encounter 'himself' there in the kitchen and not Mrs Mairi? Thomas's
brow puckered with doubt. 'Himself' seemed so stiff and
unyielding Thomas thought he would be unlikely to
understand the magic of rainbows and how compelling
was the impulse to rush outside so as to see it in its
complete glory. He stood for a few frustrated seconds, torn
between the desire to rush out as he was and risk 'himself's' displeasure, or waste precious time dressing. Mrs
Mairi had assured him that 'himself's' forbidding expression concealed a warm and gentle nature, and though
Thomas believed her, he was fearful of putting his belief to
the test so soon. Releasing the latch, he sped back to the
window. The rainbow was still visible but much of its
brilliance had paled; the encroaching mist tore it into
segments and within seconds it had disappeared.

Still exhilarated by what he had seen, Thomas crossed
to the washstand where he poured peaty brown water
from an ivy-patterned ewer into a similarly ivy-patterned
bowl. He planned to wash quickly, but when he felt the
unaccustomed softness of the water against his skin and
saw the copiousness of the soap lather, he dawdled, swirling the water into thick suds until it looked as if the bowl
was filled with melting snow.

When he had dressed he went quietly through to the
kitchen. There was no one there, but the moment he

closed the door behind him he heard the sound of Ben's tail thumping against the floor behind Sandy's chair. Lazily Ben rose, stretched and offered himself for a fussing, after which he returned to his place behind the chair. Thomas saw that the grate was full of peat ash which seemed to indicate that neither Mairi nor 'himself' were up, but as he was debating whether he should return to his own room and wait until he heard someone stirring, Mairi came through into the kitchen, fully dressed but still engaged in tying the strings of her apron.

'Why, Thomas!' she exclaimed with a broad smile. 'You're up and about awful early. I was thinking you would be staying in your bed just to celebrate not having to get up.'

Eagerly Thomas began to stammer out about seeing the rainbow but he heard the door of the bedroom open and Sandy's footsteps coming through to the kitchen. Trying to hurry out the words before 'himself' appeared, Thomas was reduced to jerky inarticulateness. Frustrated, he described with his hands the extent of the arc of the rainbow, and from his gestures and the one or two intelligible words he had managed to utter, Mairi was quick to deduce what he was trying to convey.

'You've already seen a rainbow? My! My! Thomas, then I think that must have been a special one come just to welcome you to Corrie.' She spoke with a lilting confidence. 'Do you not think that is so?' she appealed to Sandy as he came into the room.

'Aye, indeed,' Sandy supported obligingly. He slanted a flinty smile at Thomas, but Thomas was looking down at his feet and did not see it.

'Doesn't that just go to bear out what I have been telling you about this place, Thomas? This is surely rainbow land and just now is rainbow weather when the mist and the showers and the sunshine all want to take their turn at outdoing one another,' she continued. 'And if there's a pot of gold at the end of every rainbow as the Irish believe, I'm thinking Corrie must be near sinking under the weight of it all.'

Thomas watched her poke dry twigs among the peat ash in the grate. Almost immediately smoke rose from them and with a pair of bellows she blew the smoke into flame before building dry peats expertly around them.

'There now,' she said when, having checked the kettle was full, she hung it over the fire. 'We will go now and let out the hens, Thomas. The earlier they're about in the mornings, the more inclined they are to lay. Go and put on your gumboots. The ground is terrible boggy after all the rain we've had, so I doubt you'll need to be taking them off again until you're ready for your bed.'

When they opened the door to go outside they saw there was still a fine drizzle of rain. Mairi, picking up a couple of hessian sacks from a rack behind the porch door, draped one around her own shoulders and, handing the other to Thomas, bade him to do likewise. 'It will keep this bit of rain off you well enough,' she told him. More than anything she had said up to now, her calm instruction made Thomas feel that, so far as she was concerned, he had already slipped into place in the household.

Before he had left the orphanage it had been made clear to Thomas that his stay at Corrie was to be for a trial period. Only then, if he felt he could be happy with Mairi and Sandy and they with him, would the arrangement be finalized. Despite the aloofness of 'himself', it took Thomas less than a month to make up his mind that he wanted to stay with Mairi for ever at Corrie.

But it was not just his feeling for Mairi that accounted for his wish to stay. The wish was compounded of delight in the privacy that having his own bedroom gave him; of the relative freedom of life on the croft and the discovery that each day was likely to bring some new experience – an experience which, if he felt so inclined, he could probe further without fear of fuss or reprimand. Accustomed in the past to rising early at the start of a disciplined day, he still woke early, but now waking was tinged with expectation. Everything was different. Just the act of getting up was different. Now, instead of dressing immediately, he went first to look out of his bedroom window, hoping to catch a glimpse of some creature of the early dawn. Already he had been rewarded by the sight of a buzzard being mobbed by ravens; of a hedgehog snuffling around the haystacks; of a weasel sinuously exploring its way along the drystone wall; of a cat, far too large, he was sure, to be any domestic cat, streaking away up the croft in the direction of the moors.

He wanted to stay at Corrie. Of that there was no shadow of doubt in Thomas's mind. He could not bear to think that he might some day have to return to the orphanage. What he must hope for now, he told himself, was that Mairi and 'himself' should want him to stay with them. Mairi made no secret of her affection for him and of her joy in having him share her home. But 'himself' remained taciturn. Although Thomas sensed his kindness and longed to respond, Sandy so rarely spoke to him directly that when he did so, Thomas, caught offguard, became tongue-tied, too ashamed even to look up. The fear of incurring 'himself''s displeasure was a constant tremor at the back of his mind and, miserably wrestling with the problem, Thomas could think of only one solution and that was to make himself so useful around the place that 'himself' would agree to him staying for that reason alone.

5

On the first day of the new term Mairi accompanied
Thomas to the village school, where he was enrolled
among the dozen or so scholars. Not having met any of the
village children, Thomas had been dreading this day and
as a consequence was stiff with nerves and stammering
uncontrollably. The orphanage school had taught him
how cruel children can be towards affliction and he had

suffered much from the persistent, though necessarily covert, mockery and mimicry of some of the pupils. But, to his bewilderment and relief, he discovered that the Corrie children were shy of him as a stranger in their midst. Once over their shyness, they showed plainly that their interest was in himself, as a city boy, not in his affliction. Far from mocking him, they tried hard to understand him, framing their questions so a nod or a gesture was sufficient reply. When he had to struggle for speech they waited with patient understanding, displaying neither irritation nor turning away before he could complete what he was trying to say.

At the orphanage school Thomas had sought every opportunity to isolate himself from the other pupils, but here at Corrie he allowed himself to show a reciprocal interest, and the shared curiosity led to a gradual shedding of reluctance to mix with them. As he grew more relaxed in their company he found his throat muscles more yielding to his will. His stammer began to ease, giving him the hope that the day would come when he would be able to speak as fluently as they.

But it was Mairi and the seals who most helped him to overcome his stammer.

Every day, except in the stormiest weather, Mairi made a point of going down to the shore, and whenever he could Thomas liked to accompany her. Mairi seemed to regard the shore much as a supplementary store cupboard and there, in their season, she and Thomas would gather winkles to boil and eat; dulse to make soup, and carragheen for puddings. There they collected driftwood, carrying it home in rope-tied bundles or, if it was too heavy, dragging it up above high-tide line for Sandy to collect later. Sometimes they just wandered over the shingle picking up attractively coloured stones or interesting pieces of flotsam and jetsam. Other times they simply made for their favourite vantage point, a large boulder, black and shiny as a wet oilskin, which Mairi called Rabbit Rock because it resembled the shape of a crouched rabbit. There they would sit, watching and listening to the sounds of the sea and the gulls, while at the same time keeping their eyes open for the occasional school of porpoises or lone basking shark or for the more common sight of bobbing seals.

They were sitting on the Rabbit Rock one day when two young seals rose out of the water, obviously disputing the right to a large salmon which one of them held in its jaws. The dispute settled, the seals submerged. After a few minutes Mairi said, 'Let's try calling them back, shall we, Thomas?' Thomas smiled, suspecting her of joking. 'Yes, I can call seals,' she confirmed. 'Would you like to hear how I do it?' He nodded, still smiling tentatively. 'Listen then, and keep watch,' she told him. Putting her hands to her mouth and lifting her normally soft voice, she startled Thomas by sending out a loud ululating cry, amplifying and directing the sound by the movement of her fingers. Repeatedly she called, and Thomas, scrutinizing every joggle of a wave, perceived at last the shiny, dark blob of a seal's head emerge from the water. Thomas turned to gape at Mairi in surprise and delight. She continued to call and soon the head of a second seal appeared close to the first one.

'They've seen us,' Mairi cried. The seals seemed to be watching them curiously. 'Now, Thomas, see if you can imitate me and call them in closer.'

Irresolutely Thomas put his hands up to his mouth. 'Go on!' Mairi urged. 'Take a deep, deep breath and then push it out with all your strength.' Thomas did as she said but his call came out feebly. 'Louder!' commanded Mairi. She put a fist on his abdomen. 'A great big breath now,' she instructed. Thomas breathed deeply and felt a kind of hiccough in his chest as his throat swelled and the sound he was striving to make burst freely from his mouth. Immediately his hands dropped loosely as if the effort had weakened him. The seals stayed where they were, watching them but not coming any closer inshore. 'Try again!' Mairi could not disguise the satisfaction in her voice. When for a second time Thomas's call boomed out, the seals submerged, but just as he was beginning to feel disappointed, they bobbed up again, discernibly nearer the shore.

'No, not again!' Mairi said as Thomas, with growing confidence, was about to put his hands again to his mouth. 'The tide's going out so they won't come in closer for fear of getting stranded.'

The seals were still visible, bobbing up and submerging as they ranged along the coast, when Mairi decided it was time to return to the cottage. The third time Thomas turned to look over his shoulder towards the sea Mairi said, 'Did you know that some folks believe you should always tell your sorrows and joys to the seals?' Thomas shook his head. 'They do indeed. They say the seals take messages to the seal king. If you tell them good news there's a great rejoicing among seals everywhere.' Mairi paused. Thomas looked up at her inquiringly. 'And if it's sad news,' she went on, 'the seals ask the seal king to help you. And they say he does; that the very next seal you see will bring you a sense of great comfort. That's why you should always tell the seals when someone you love has died because the seals are supposed to keep in touch with the spirits of those who have passed on and can give them messages about things you'd like them to know about.'

Thomas regarded her gravely. 'D'-d'-you b-believe these things?' he asked.

'Yes, I think I do,' Mairi replied with equal gravity, though she was careful to keep her fingers crossed. 'I believe if you were to ask the seals to help you get rid of your stammer then they would.'

Since she had come to live in Corrie, Mairi had heard many stories of people who were reputed not only to be able to call seals but also to communicate with them. She had heard about seals taking human shapes; of women having seal lovers and being carried off to sea. They were part of the folklore of Corrie along with the stories of 'wee folk' and 'water horses'. By this time Thomas had probably heard them too, but when she had told him she herself could call seals, her claim had been the result of a sudden impulse which itself had sprung from a desire to find some way of helping Thomas combat his stammer. She was familiar with seal noises as groups of them frequently hauled out on the skerries beyond the bay where they conferred and grumbled as they jockeyed for the best positions on the rocks. All she had to do was to try to imitate them. When the first seal had appeared she had been even more surprised than Thomas. She knew it was no more than coincidence, but all the same, when the second seal bobbed up she wondered if her mimicry was being successful.

When Thomas had summoned his own throat to produce the sound, she had been so overjoyed that on the spur of the moment she had invented the story of the seal king and seal messengers, hoping that if she could encourage him to use his voice to call regularly to the seals, he might find it easier to control his stammering. To her delight the strategy appeared to work. Often, after he had come home from school, Thomas, without saying where he was going, would disappear for half an hour and would come back bringing the smell of the sea with him. One evening when he returned he confided stumblingly, 'The seals c-came. I asked th-them t-to tell my G-Gran how happy I w-was here.' He and Mairi exchanged a shy conspiratorial glance and Mairi exonerated herself from any vestige of guilt over her deception.

Gran was the only mother Thomas had ever known, his real mother having died before he was three months old. That much Mairi had learned from the orphanage records, but when she and Thomas were alone together, and as his speech improved, she had, by reminiscing about her own orphanage experiences, gently drawn him into recalling memories of his own childhood. The memories had come fitfully, usually sparked off by something she had said, but from them she had pieced together a fairly complete story.

He appeared to have had a happy if fairly repressed childhood, his Gran having been a loving but often irritable and sharp-voiced guardian, not much given to any display of affection. When he had discovered that other children of his age had someone they called their 'Mum' and he had asked why he couldn't call her 'Mum' instead of 'Gran', she had explained that she was not his 'Mum' and had told him gently enough about his mother. The same had not happened when he had asked why he had no one to call 'Dad'. Then the snapped reply had been, 'He was a bad man. I will not speak of him!' With timid persistence strengthened by yearning, Thomas had pursued his questioning, wanting to know how bad his father had been, but his Gran had glared at him, angrier than he had ever seen her. 'He didn't want your mother and he didn't want you when you were born,' she had told him and Thomas, cringing at the terrible disclosure, had never again felt tempted to ask about his father.

Shortly after his fifth birthday and only two days before he was looking forward to hanging up his stocking for Santa Claus to fill, Thomas had been wakened by hearing his Gran's voice calling to him from across the narrow landing that divided their bedrooms. Running quickly into the old lady's room, he had found her fighting for breath and, between gasps, trying to tell him to run and get the next-door neighbour. As soon as the neighbour had arrived she had sent Thomas to call yet another neighbour and shortly afterwards the nurse had arrived. Thomas remembered being worried, but since he had been told he must stay downstairs he had sat in the Christmas-garlanded kitchen trying to give all his attention to his toys. He was there to see the doctor arrive and to see him leave a few minutes later. Thomas's worry eased. A doctor would have to stay a long time with someone who was really ill, he had reasoned. The fact that the doctor had left so soon after arriving meant that Gran was going to be all right again. He had worked out in his own mind what must have happened. His Gran had been doing the Christmas baking the previous evening and she was always popping bits of whatever she was mixing into her mouth as she worked. She must have got one of the bits stuck in her throat, he reckoned, and that was why she had been gasping so much. Now the doctor had been able to remove whatever it had been and she would soon be well again. He could imagine how she would chide herself for having been so careless. Except for low murmurings and soft treads upstairs, the house had settled back into its usual quiet, which seemed to Thomas to bear out his theory. Any minute now he expected to be told he could now go upstairs and see his Gran. But the first neighbour had come down and explained that Gran was sleeping and the doctor had said she mustn't be disturbed. Shortly afterwards the second neighbour and the nurse had come down, and the second neighbour had taken him to have dinner with herself and her two children who, though they sometimes bullied him, he counted among his playmates.

He had stayed on for tea but he had begun to worry again about his Gran. He told his neighbour he must go back to the house, but she had said no, not yet; Gran would still be sleeping. After her own two children had been told to go to bed she had drawn him to her gently and told him that he would have to stay for a few more days because his Gran had died and was now on her way to Heaven.

Thomas hadn't believed her. At that age his ideas about death had been misty and confused. People who died vanished so you never saw them again. Thomas was quite sure his Gran hadn't vanished. Gran was asleep in her own bed in her own bedroom. Death happened to people who had accidents or who had been taken to hospital because they were poorly. His Gran hadn't had an accident and only last night she had been teaching him to sing 'Good King Wenceslaus' while she baked mince pies. He hadn't been able to believe that someone could bake mince pies one night and then die the very next morning. Somebody had made a mistake. Gran would wake up again soon and tell everybody off for being such fusspots. But all the same, he wanted to run back to the house just to make sure. Again the neighbour had restrained him. Granny's house was now locked up. He would not be able to get inside. He remembered he had cried then, not because he had come to believe his Granny was dead but because he knew it was expected of him.

Still only half convinced that Gran would not appear and briskly take him back home with her, he went numbly through the Christmas celebrations. But then, two days after Christmas, the elder of his two playmates had confided that while Thomas had been taken shopping he had seen a van arrive at his Gran's house and some men had carried away his Granny in a big black box. Thomas admitted to having started to scream out loud then, partly because of the dreadful image that formed in his mind, partly because he now knew that what everyone had been

A Shine of Rainbows

telling him was true. He was never going to see his Gran
again.

His next memory was of the minister, a restless little
man, a bit like a blackbird, Thomas recalled, who had set
him on his lap telling him he must try not to be sad any
more because his Gran was now resting safely in the arms
of a loving Jesus. Thomas's pale cheeks had reddened
with shame as he confessed to Mairi how he had turned on
the minister, pummelling at his face and crying that Jesus
couldn't be loving like people said. That he must be cruel
because he wanted people packed in big black boxes
before they were sent to him.

When he had been told he was soon going to live in a big
house where there would be lots of other children for him
to play with, his first idea had been to get into his Gran's
house some way or other and barricade himself in so that
no one could take him away. He described the old house
vividly. His own little bedroom with the peg rug Gran had
made; the kitchen with its big range; the sturdy wooden
table on which he could spread out his drawing books
when Gran wasn't using it for baking or under which he
could take his toys and pretend he was in a castle or in a
tent in the desert. He spoke fondly of the red paisley-
cushioned sofa which always seemed to be holding out its
arms invitingly; he remembered the rows of plates, shining like friendly faces on the shelves of the big dresser
which Gran had always kept so well polished it seemed
every firelight flame was reflected by the dark wood.

His playmate, eager to be first with the information,
had told him, 'It's not really a big house you're going to at
all. It's an orphanage.' He had spoken the word gloat-
ingly, Thomas said, as if it was the only three-syllabled
word he knew. 'Children who haven't got mums and dads
are sent to orphanages when nobody else wants them.'

Until that moment Thomas had been wanting to get

away from his temporary home as soon as he could, but anyone's home was then, it seemed to him, better than an orphanage. He remembered working up the courage to ask if he could stay on but there had been so many reasons against it, it was plain even to him that they simply didn't want him. The neighbour had cried a little but it hadn't convinced Thomas. He knew it was because he didn't belong. Remembering about his father, it seemed that there was no one to want him now that his Gran was dead.

The morning the car had come to collect him he had noticed a furniture van outside his Gran's house and some men loading the big dresser into the van. He told Mairi he had thought then that Gran must be missing her dresser so much she had asked Jesus if it could go to Heaven with her. He'd wondered if he could hide inside it and go and be with Gran again. But they were sure to see him and prevent him, he'd thought. Resolving to be brave and not watch any more, he was turning away but just then he caught sight of two more men carrying out the paisley-patterned sofa. He'd felt a sudden urge to take a last look at it before it was taken away and ducking from his escort he had started to run towards the van. A shout of laughter made him pull up short and to his horror he had seen that one of the arms of the sofa had been broken off. The man who was laughing was waving it about for his mate to see. 'The old sofa's no more than firewood,' he had called as he tossed the arm into the back of the van. Someone had come and led Thomas back to the car then – the car that was going to take him to what he thought of as yet another place of 'not belonging'.

Of his life at the orphanage Thomas spoke little. He remembered being ill shortly after he arrived there and he thought the illness had been quite a serious one because afterwards he'd been sent for a time to a convalescent home near the sea. He thought he must always have had a tendency to stammer because Gran had sometimes reproved him about it, but he seemed to think it had got much worse as a result of his illness. He couldn't remember having been teased about stammering before, but as soon as he returned to the orphanage and had begun to attend the orphanage school the teasing and the taunting had begun, so much so that he had come to dread having to speak at all. It had been decided he must wear spectacles too and he'd hated that. They made him clumsy, he said, because they never stayed in place on his nose. He appeared to retain no pleasant memories of his life at the orphanage save of a brief friendship with a girl of his own age who had also stammered but who all too soon had been whisked away by adoptive parents.

Mairi, who, throughout her own childhood and adolescence, had known at first hand the difficulties some children faced in adjusting to communal life, was deeply touched. Sometimes, when Thomas had broken off suddenly in the middle of retailing some memory, as if he found it too painful to recall, she longed for his further confidence. But at no time did she press him. As much as he told her, she felt, he needed to tell someone. It was as if he wanted the telling to ease the lacerating awareness of being unwanted which was still gnawing at his young mind. Mairi, sensing it was also, however unwittingly, an appeal against further hurt, yearned to reassure him but she knew from experience that children who have been badly hurt do not easily accept such assurances. She could only wait to convince him until he had absorbed the permanence of Corrie as his home and learned trust in his own way.

Once or twice Thomas asked her about her own life in an orphanage and Mairi had told him that, since she had never known her parents nor any relatives, nor indeed any other life she had been content enough. 'What you've never had you never miss,' she said lightly. But when she had met his puzzled eyes she had admitted to sometimes being aware of a sense of deprivation, as when those children who could recall a pre-orphanage life swapped wistful memories which gave glimpses of what a home might be. She told him how, when she had been very young, one girl had disclosed that whenever one of her teeth came out she would wrap it in a piece of paper and put it under the pillow for the tooth fairy who would then come and take the tooth and leave a sixpence in exchange. Mairi had never heard of such a happening but she remembered when her next tooth came out to pop it under her pillow as the other girl had said. But it seemed tooth fairies didn't visit orphanages because the tooth was still there the next morning and the next and the next until eventually she had thrown it out of the window in a fit of rage and disappointment.

While she talked she was mixing scones in a bowl on the table and when she looked up she saw that Thomas was watching her sombrely.

'Well,' she said as she wiped her floury hands on a cloth, 'that's all I can tell you about my early days for the moment.' She was gathering up the cooking utensils when Thomas said, so quietly that she barely heard him, 'I wish you were really my Mum.'

His words brought such a leap of joy to her heart that for a moment it was she who felt tongue-tied. 'Let's make ourselves believe that's what I am,' she suggested. Her voice shook a little but her smile was steady.

'If I c-could c-call you M-Mum it would be easier to b-believe you really are my M-Mum,' he said diffidently.

The words were so much those she wanted to hear that she feared for an instant she might sound too gushing. 'Then why not call me Mum,' she said. 'I'd like that.'

'Truly?'

She looked directly at him and saw the blush rising to his cheeks. His eyes glowed as his lips began to lift in a smile that spread ecstatically over his face. 'Truly,' she said.

'M-Mum!' He spoke the word tentatively at first. Mairi's smile was encouraging. 'Mum?' he said again as if testing the feel of the word on his tongue.

'It sounds fine, doesn't it?' They looked at each other as if together they had made some precious discovery. Thomas noticed that one of Mairi's hands was on her heart.

'D-Does your heart hurt you?' His voice was anxious.

'Sometimes. But only when I'm happy,' she said.

Thomas stood up and going into the porch opened the outer door and stood looking out at the weather. She heard him pulling on his gumboots and taking down his jacket from the peg. He did not say where he was going and she did not ask him. She guessed he was going to tell the seals.

6

Thomas, zealously carrying out his intention of earning the approval of 'himself', made determined efforts to help whenever he could around the croft and house. He worked willingly beside Mairi at the potato planting, sometimes wondering as he spaced the seed potatoes in the furrows already dug by Sandy whether he would still be at Corrie to help eat the results of his labours. And when he worked at the peats, helping Mairi lift and arrange the cut peats into what she called 'castles' to dry off before being finally built into the large stacks which would stand firm against the winter storms, he let his mind race ahead to create a picture of 'himself' striding down the croft carrying a well-packed creel of the dry peats; of Mairi deftly placing the peats on the fire; of the way the flames immediately ignited the myriad of rough fibres, first nibbling at them and then leaping to devour and transform them into glowing embers that seemed to him to breathe as they burned. He saw himself poking crab claws into the embers to roast for a tasty evening snack.

He volunteered to look after the hens, not just taking over the feeding of them but also the cleaning of their shed, which he did cheerfully and regularly without the need for reminders. Believing Sandy despised him for his puniness, he took upon himself the task of carrying water from the well, struggling sometimes and causing Mairi many a secret but proud smile because in his earnest desire to prove his strength he tended to fill the pails too full.

He learned to milk the cows and when the time came for the first of the season's calvings and he was allowed to be present in the byre, he watched with as much goggle-eyed concern as the cow herself while the calf was born. A few days later he was feeding the calf, offering his fingers as a substitute teat while it drank the warm milk from the pail.

When the sheep-shearing time came he joined the other children, sometimes helping them to keep the sheep from straying out of the fold but more often watching the shearing itself, intrigued by the way the newly shorn-off fleeces stayed sheep-like as if they had a separate life of their own, so much so that he found himself wincing when they were roughly gathered up and kicked and rolled and thumped into bundles ready for dispatch to the mainland mills for spinning into wool.

It seemed to Thomas a little unreal when Mairi later consulted with him over the colour they wanted the wool to be dyed, and when, weeks later, the carrier delivered two sacks of spun wool which Mairi tipped out onto the table he handled the thick skeins, winding them speculatively around his arms and draping them over his shoulders. When, after several periods of busy knitting, Mairi presented him with socks and pullover knitted from that same wool he felt he could truly claim to belong to Corrie.

After school and during the holiday Mairi encouraged Thomas to seek the company of the other children of the village. As a consequence he joined them in their search for gulls' eggs, practising the trick of testing the eggs for freshness in a can of water. At other times they would take him fishing and once he had been initiated into the intricacies of baiting a line he soon became as expert as they at hooking the small brown trout which abounded in quiet pools in the burns and in bringing in the bronze-gold sea wrasse which populated the deep water around the rocks of the shore.

When a hint of autumn brought the promise of ripening nuts and purpling brambles, Thomas was often one of a group of eager children who, armed with stout sticks and with a lunch 'piecey' in their pocket, would go off to spend a day among the random hazel trees and tangle of sprawling brambles which, when contrasted with the barrenness of the moors, could legitimately be described as a wood.

The more he was in the company of the crofter children the more like them he became in appearance. His downcast expression was slowly replaced by one of cheerful alertness; his spindly body began to manifest signs of increasing sturdiness; his hair, no longer cropped by an over-efficient barber but kept trimmed by Mairi's scissors, was now rarely covered and, responding to the challenge of the wind and rain, showed signs of growing as thick and shaggy as that of a highland calf. And almost without his noticing it his eyesight improved.

When Thomas had been at the orphanage the supervisor had insisted on him wearing spectacles at all times, not simply for reading. Puzzled but compliant, Thomas had done so and in time had ceased to remember that until he was made to wear them he'd been just as able as other children to see the whole length of a street and even to see the birds fluttering among the trees across the park. When he began to attend the Corrie school he was sensitive to the fact that he was the only pupil who wore spectacles. Indeed, he soon found that except for Mairi, who needed them when she was doing close work in the lamplight, he was the only person in Corrie who needed spectacles. The fact that he did so impressed the other scholars. Why? they wanted to know, and when he replied that he could not see without them they made no secret of their bafflement. They begged, in turn, to try them on, peering myopically when they did so and exclaiming how blurred everything appeared. Without any intention of making fun of him, they sometimes withheld his spectacles, refusing to give them back until he had managed to identify to their satisfaction objects which they were sure he ought to be able to see. When he had done so, they gave their unanimous opinion that he could see almost as well as they and was therefore stupid to wear them. Anyway, they warned, it wasn't safe for him to wear them when he was out scrambling and climbing because he, like them, often took a tumble. He could easily smash his glasses and perhaps run the risk of blinding himself. So, in their artless way, they reasoned, and Thomas, eager to earn their approval, was tempted to take their advice. There was, however, an even stronger inducement to Thomas to try to manage without his spectacles.

The Corrie climate produced a superabundance of

misty days and when he was outdoors Thomas found he had so often to take off his spectacles and wipe them clear that it became less frustrating for him to leave them off on misty days and try his best to see without them. When he was down at the shore calling and keeping a lookout for seals, it was not just mist but salt spray which coated the lenses, so again he preferred to take them off and concentrate on seeing as much as he could without their aid. The persistent staring into far distances brought noticeable results. His weak sight gradually strengthened; his range of vision stretched, bringing distant images more sharply into focus. Thomas himself was slow to recognize the improvement and sometimes it was not until he put his hand in his pocket and found his spectacles there that he realized he had not been wearing them.

His sight was still less good than that of other children. He could not, like them, easily distinguish the shapes of deer and sheep on the hills, but then, he accepted, he was disadvantaged. As Mairi explained, Corrie children were born with their eyes looking up to the hills; town children with their eyes looking up to the nearest lamppost. Thomas was convinced that if he persevered the day would come when he could dispense with his spectacles completely.

The change in Thomas was not lost on Sandy.

'I wouldn't have believed it possible,' he remarked to Mairi one night after Thomas had gone to bed. She looked at him inquiringly, knowing full well what he meant but nevertheless wanting him to put it into words. 'The boy,' said Sandy. 'You wouldn't know he was the same child that you brought here.'

'Didn't I say that would happen?' she retorted. 'Now you've seen what Corrie has done for him, do you wonder I wanted to bring him here?'

'Is it Corrie that's made him what he is? Had

you nothing to do with it then?' His tone was ironic.

'A little perhaps.' She paused. 'You've noticed he calls me Mum now?'

'I had so.'

'You don't mind?'

'Why should I?' He darted a look at her. 'What does he call me when he speaks of me?'

'Just "himself". I think he knows you wouldn't have wanted him to call you Sandy so he just refers to you as "himself".'

Sandy grunted. 'Good enough,' he said.

Mairi gave him an anxious look. 'Dear,' she began, 'I wish you'd try and talk to Thomas more than you do. Oh, yes, I know,' she forestalled his protest. 'You've said before you can get no response from him but, you see, he's not nearly so nervous now as he used to be. Perhaps if you tried telling him about what sort of day you'd had on the hill or what sort of fishing you'd had; oh, about anything you've seen or heard that might interest him . . . ' Her voice trailed away as if she was daunted by the expression on her husband's face.

'You know fine I've never been one for much talk, Mairi,' he reminded her. There was an edge of finality in his voice which Mairi chose to ignore.

'Yes, I do know,' she replied. 'But what I'm asking is for you to try. Thomas would just love to be able to talk to you, but he can't. You could talk to Thomas if you chose, but you won't.' She made a small gesture of helplessness. 'I believe it would help him a lot if you could get to know each other better. . . . He's not stupid Sandy, dear. Mistress McLeod says he is one of her best scholars.'

'Sharing the same house with him all this time, do I not know him well enough, then?'

'No!' Mairi's voice rose a little. 'You don't know him. You won't either until you learn to share other things with him. Not just a house.' She was leaning towards him earnestly and her knitting slid off her lap. Bending forward to retrieve it, she missed seeing the dismissive twitch of her husband's mouth. He rose and, picking up the half empty peat bucket and the hurricane lamp, went out to the peat shed. As the door closed behind him, Mairi sighed and resumed her knitting.

Sandy topped up the pail with dry peats and then leaned back against the stack, meditating sourly on his wife's request. He had gone along with her idea of taking the strange boy into her home. He had tried, so far as he could, to make the boy feel welcome. He was resolved to continue to wait patiently for the response which Mairi repeatedly assured him would one day come from Thomas, but not even for Mairi would he be able to shed his natural taciturnity. His dour, religious parents, mistrusting what they termed 'a flowing tongue', had suppressed in their children the slightest tendency to talkativeness. 'Wise men think – fools talk,' his father had been fond of quoting and, having absorbed his teaching from earliest childhood, Sandy knew that brevity of speech was too deeply ingrained in him for him to change now. He stayed for some minutes, letting the sounds of the night soothe his disgruntled feelings.

'Indeed, I thought you must have fallen asleep out there,' Mairi reproached him when he got back to the kitchen. She reached for the teapot and poured him a mug of tea.

Sandy put down the pail of peats and blew out the hurricane lamp. As if he had not heard her he said, 'I believe we're in for a fine spell of weather.'

Mairi sipped her tea thoughtfully. 'I was thinking I would go across to the mainland tomorrow,' she said. 'It's keeping calm enough and the bus has been getting back fairly early the last few days.'

'See and don't tire yourself then,' Sandy warned. The last time she had been across to the mainland she had come back pale and exhausted.

'No, I'll not do that but, you see, it is Thomas's birthday shortly and I'm wanting to get him a darra of his own so he can go fishing.' Sandy thought there was a slight note of challenge in her voice.

'It's a wee bit late in the year to be buying tackle, surely,' he pointed out.

'Not too late, though,' she returned. 'Young Shamus was showing Thomas a good lythe he'd caught only the other evening when he was out fishing with his brother. I think Thomas is hoping that if he has tackle of his own Shamus's brother might take him fishing too.'

'Maybe,' said Sandy flatly, aware that she was obliquely censuring him for never having offered to take Thomas fishing himself.

The next morning, after he had seen Mairi away on the bus, Sandy prepared to go and lift his lobster creels. Thomas always took a 'piece' to school for his lunch and since, when he came home from school, he would see to the feeding of the hens, Sandy reckoned that he himself would not need to get back to the cottage much before the time Mairi would be returning. For some time he had been planning to collect a good plank of wood which had been washed ashore in a cove a little way along the coast, but either the weather had been too stormy or else he had been anxious to get back to his sheep. Today the tide and the weather were favourable and he need be in no hurry. On his way back from lifting the creels he would at last be able to pick up the wood. So he had planned, but when he nosed the boat into the cove he saw a young seal pup lying above the tide line. Leaving Ben aboard, he moored the boat and waded ashore. The seal lifted its head, its big eyes following his every movement as he carried the plank down to the tide line and loaded it onto the boat. In general Sandy considered it best to leave any seal pups well alone since the mother seal was likely to be in the offing ready to tend it when she felt it necessary, but there was something about this pup that troubled him. Going back, he circled the seal deliberately, assessing its condition. Approaching closer, he worked his hands under its body, urging it towards the water. Weakly the pup tried to protest at his handling it, but its head sank slowly down to rest on the shingle. Sandy, suspecting it was weak from starvation, went back to the boat thinking he would try catching one or two fish to feed it, but as he started the engine he thought of Thomas. Mairi had confided the story of the seals and of how Thomas went often to call to them and recalling it made him also remember her plea of the previous evening. He looked at the horizon and at the amount of light on the water by which means he judged that Thomas should be home from school. Instead of steering the boat out to where he might find fish, Sandy turned the bow to head homeward.

Thomas, having fed the hens, was trying his hand at building up part of a drystone wall which had collapsed. He had seen 'himself' coming up from the shore but pretended not to notice.

'Thomas!' The stone Thomas was lifting slipped from his hands as he looked apprehensively towards Sandy. 'Come now! There's something you must see.' Incredulously Thomas saw 'himself' beckoning to him before turning back and making in the direction of the shore. Half bemused by what was happening, Thomas followed him.

Out in the bay Sandy caught fish and then turned the boat towards the cove where the seal pup still lay helplessly, but when he offered the fish the pup would not take it.

'Stay there!' he told Thomas and going back to the boat he returned with a pair of thick gloves. Thomas's eyes were wide with inquiry. 'He's not used to feeding himself. We'll need to teach him or he'll starve. You don't want that, do you?' Sandy spoke in clipped sentences. Thomas shook his head. 'Right. Keep a hold of one of those small fish and, when I force his mouth open, ram it in quickly.' Eagerly Thomas grasped a fish and held it ready while 'himself' held the seal's mouth open with a stave of wood. The fish disappeared down the seal's throat and Thomas pushed in another and then another. The seal squirmed as if the food had instantly restored its strength.

'Leave him now and come away home.'

Reluctantly Thomas followed Sandy down to the boat. He wanted to ask if the seal would survive but though the words reached his throat he could not speak them. All he could do was to sit and look miserably back at the seal.

When Mairi came home and Thomas told her what had happened she listened thoughtfully. As soon as Sandy came in she asked, 'Has it a chance, d'you think?'

'Maybe.' He sounded noncommittal. 'Thomas can come with me tomorrow when he gets back from school and we'll try feeding it again.' He was looking at Mairi, so did not see the look of delight that spread over Thomas's face. 'It should soon learn to take the fish from us.'

'I hope the weather stays calm for it,' said Mairi. 'A storm might wash it back to sea.'

'If it starts to look bad, we'll maybe net the pup and bring it back to the shore here so it'll be easier for Thomas to feed it,' Sandy told her.

Thomas stared at Sandy. When they had both bent over the seal pup together Thomas's questioning eyes had seen for the first time the tenderness behind 'himself's' grim expression, but he was still hardly able to believe he was hearing what he thought he heard. He looked at Mairi and then back again at Sandy. But they were looking at each other and in their expressions there was something too deep for Thomas to understand.

They had fed the seal pup for some days, Sandy catching the fish while he was out attending to his lobster creels and leaving enough under the floorboards of the boat to keep fresh, ready to be taken to the cove as soon as Thomas came home from school. The pup quickly learned to recognize them, moving its head curiously from side to side as it watched them wade ashore, squirming and making little noises, like cut-off yawns, as they approached. It was not long before it was taking fish from them without Sandy having first to force open its jaws and when they left to return to the boat it seemed to Thomas, at any rate, that the pup watched their departure forlornly. And then one evening when they arrived at the cove there was no seal there waiting for them.

'Likely it's decided it can fend for itself,' said Sandy briefly and headed the boat back towards the bay.

Thomas was not as dismayed as he might have been over the seal pup's disappearance, Mairi having warned him that as soon as it felt strong enough it would probably make its way back to the sea to join its own kind. He was more dismayed at the thought of there being no more trips with 'himself', for though few words had been exchanged between them while they were together there had been communication of a sort; a kind of swift interpretation of each other's thoughts that was like the beginnings of understanding. Thomas, pondering over it, was even more inclined to believe in 'seal magic'.

7

In Corrie there was no tradition of birthday celebrations; birthday cakes and the giving of presents, even to young children, were alien practices indulged in by the feckless people of the mainland towns and cities. The staid crofters of Corrie were not disposed to waste time and money on observing such useless customs.

Mairi, who during her years in service had often been

involved in such celebrations, gave Thomas his birthday present darra before he left for school that morning. When he came home in the evening it was to see the table spread with Mairi's newest tablecloth in the centre of which there stood a round, pink-iced sponge cake.

Thomas gasped with pleasure at the sight. 'Is that for me, Mum?'

Mairi nodded. 'That's the best I could manage in the way of decorations though,' she told him flippantly. 'No one's ever heard of birthday cake candles in this part of the world.' She laughed.

When she had spoken to the bus driver about the possibility of his getting her some cake candles he had been so mystified by her request that, dubious as to what he might contrive to find for her, she had thought it wiser not to pursue the matter. When she had inquired at the few shops the mainland village boasted she had been met with suspicious refusals. They sold only standard household candles, they told her frostily, implying by their tone that anything other than a plain candle was, in their eyes, associated with papism. Thinking about their attitude as she was returning home on the bus, she wondered wryly how she had ever dared imagine that cheerful baubles like cake candles could have sneaked, however slyly, into such a stronghold of Calvinism.

Not really seeking an alternative but with the thought lingering at the back of her mind, she had spotted in a sheltered patch of the croft a few remaining plumes of bog cotton which had not been shredded by the autumn gales. She had plucked nine of them that morning and had pushed their thin stiff stalks into the cake as a substitute for the candles.

Thomas was still staring at the cake as if he doubted it was real. 'They look m-much nicer than c-candles,' he assured Mairi with such feeling that she had to believe him. 'They look like silver flags around a castle.' The little smile that was always hovering around Mairi's mouth broadened to embrace him in its warmth.

'You do make me feel clever, saying things like that,' she said.

'You are c-clever.' He loved to see her smile at him as she was smiling now. He loved it even more when it was something he had said that caused the smile. 'You're cleverer than all the other women in Corrie,' he declared staunchly and immediately rushed to get on with the task of giving the hens their evening feed.

On his way back he was met by the strong hunger-making smells of toasting flour and roasting meat and entering the kitchen he saw Mairi bending over the range testing the tenderness of a dish of cooked skart before sliding it back into the oven. The smell of the rich gravy filled the kitchen. Thomas almost groaned with the hunger that the combination of smells aroused in him. He fidgeted around for some minutes before settling down with a book, but all the time his ears were alert to catch the sound of 'himself's' return since not until then would they begin their evening meal.

When Sandy did get back he brought a pail half full of large crab claws. Thomas's eyes gleamed. What a feast! Skart pie, potatoes, birthday cake and now roast crab claws to look forward to! He had his chair drawn up to the table before Sandy had taken off his boots.

The birthday cake was half eaten by the time they got round to roasting the crab claws and while Thomas sat on the hearth rug, having as usual claimed the job of cracking the cooked claws as they came out of the fire, Sandy watched him secretly, contrasting the pale limp-fingered hands of the boy who had first arrived with the firm, tanned hands which now grasped the poker and wielded it with such confidence. His gaze shifted to Mairi. How much she had done for this boy! How sensitive of his needs she had been! How gently she encouraged him! There were times when, acknowledging in his own mind how little he had contributed to Thomas's transformation, he was pricked by uneasiness. True, he had come to accept the boy as a permanent presence in the household, neither criticizing nor interfering with any of the plans Mairi chose to make for him. He had provided for him ungrudgingly, but he knew that everything he had done had been with Mairi's happiness in mind rather than out of concern for the boy. And there was no doubting Mairi's happiness. The coming of Thomas appeared to have driven away any last shreds of grief over her childlessness. Only occasionally did Sandy notice the lines of strain beneath her blithe expression and then he would wonder anxiously whether the responsibility was proving more of a strain than she realized.

The weeks went by and Thomas, impatient to try out his new darra, was constantly thwarted. The short winter days left no light for him to go fishing after he had returned home from school and the weather that winter seemed to reserve most of its savagery for the days when there was no school. He had to console himself by leaning over the dinghies when he was down at the shore, running his hands along their gunwales and imagining how it would feel to row out into the bay, lower his darra over the side and perhaps return home with a string of fresh-caught fish.

Sandy owned three boats: *Mairi*, which was the motor boat he used for lobster fishing and which was moored in a miniature lagoon formed by a narrow indentation of the coast, and two dinghies, *Puffin* and *Beulah*, which he kept on the shore at the bottom of the croft. *Puffin*, which he had recently purchased, was small and light enough for Mairi to be able to manage by herself; *Beulah* was big and husky, needing a man's strength to haul her up and down the shore and to wield the heavy oars.

With the coming of spring there were calmer spells and lighter evenings, but then the work of the croft occupied most of the hours of daylight and Thomas had to accept that not until the interval between the end of spring planting and the beginning of the harvest would Mairi be able to keep her promise to take him fishing.

On one of the first fine evenings, after the spring work was complete and while Sandy was away inspecting the herd of highland cattle which stayed permanently out on the moors, Mairi said, 'I think we should try out your darra this evening, don't you, Thomas?' Quick as a shot Thomas bounded into his bedroom and, returning with his darra neatly rolled, followed Mairi down to the shore. Together they launched *Puffin* and, taking the oars, Mairi rowed out into the bay. They did not go beyond the bay because, as Mairi pointed out, at certain stages of the tide there was a fierce tide rip in which a small boat could easily be caught and swept out to sea unless there was an exceptionally strong rower to pull against it. So they stayed within the stretch of sea that was held protectively by the arms of the bay and, when they reached what Mairi thought was a likely spot for fishing, she rested on her oars and told Thomas to lower his darra. She had chosen well. Thomas felt the darra quiver almost immediately as a fish investigated the coloured feathers on its hooks. He shouted excitedly as the darra became heavier. Telling him to haul it in, Mairi shipped her oars and hurried to help pull in the line, unhooking the fish before their writhing could turn the line into a tangle that would take them the rest of the evening to unravel. Again Thomas lowered the darra, again the fish flung themselves onto the hooks. But when he lowered a third time the line hung limp. Evidently either *Puffin* had drifted off the shoal or else the fish changed direction, since though they continued trying they caught no more fish on the hooks.

'By the time we've gutted all these and filleted those we want to eat, it'll be time for our supper and our beds,' Mairi said, pulling the boat round and rowing slowly towards the shore. 'Anyway, Thomas, d'you realize if we were to go on catching fish at that rate we'd be near enough to sinking poor *Puffin*.'

Thomas looked down at the silvery fish lying in the bottom of the boat. 'I don't think I'm going to be able to eat more than two of them. Leastways not tonight,' he said mournfully.

Mairi chuckled. 'And that's having eyes bigger than your belly,' she teased.

They gutted the fish, standing at the water's edge and flinging the entrails to the hovering gulls, and when they had finished they put aside what fish they wanted for themselves and threw the rest into the big barrel in which Sandy kept his lobster bait.

'Well, Thomas,' said Mairi as they walked back to the cottage. 'Are you happy now you've well and truly christened your darra?'

Thomas beamed at her. Her hand was resting in the region of her heart as she walked and he knew, because she had already told him, that meant she too was very happy.

In the few weeks that followed and whenever it was calm enough to go fishing the pattern of the evening was repeated. Thomas soon learned how to row, first by taking one oar while Mairi took the other and then progressing rapidly under Mairi's coaching until he could take both oars and also backwater and turn as necessary. The fishing was not always so good as it was that first night but when it was slow they simply let *Puffin* drift, moving the oars sporadically to keep her from heading towards the mouth of the bay. And while they drifted they sometimes sang to try to lure back the seals which seemed to have deserted the bay during the warmer months of summer; or they watched the seabirds busy about their own fishing; or, when the beauty of the night tempted them to linger longer than usual, they shielded their eyes from the glow of the fiery sunset so as to peer down into the violet depths of the water.

But inexorably harvest time crept up on them and again the days were filled with the demands of the croft. Thomas enjoyed helping to gather in the sweet-scented hay and the mealy-smelling corn, but since he had discovered the thrill of fishing he tended to resent the fact that Mairi was too tired after her day's work to be beguiled into taking him fishing in the evening. He could understand her tiredness; he was often aware of feeling tired himself after only a few hours of strenuous harvesting, but given the chance to go fishing he would instantly have forgotten his tiredness.

It was on a day towards the end of the harvest and as he was getting ready to go to school that Mairi reminded him that in two weeks' time the officials from the Adoption Society were expected to visit Corrie, bringing with them the necessary documents which when signed would endorse his legal adoption. Thomas had not needed the reminder. She had first mentioned the proposed visit and the purpose of it three months previously, since when he had wakened each morning with the thought of it gladdening his mind. Throwing her a smile over his shoulder, he dashed off to school, warmed by the thought that in fourteen days he would belong to his Corrie home as securely as other Corrie children belonged to theirs. In fourteen days' time 'himself' would become legally his 'Dad', but Thomas wondered more wishfully than hopefully if the day would come when he would be encouraged to address Sandy as such.

The day was grey and by the time school was over lowering cloud had wreathed the land with a drearily persistent drizzle. As the pupils dashed off towards their homes, one of them stopped to observe, 'Ach, I believe it would be good fishing this evening and seeing the day's not been fit for any work in the harvest he'll maybe fancy going fishing.' He darted off purposefully and Thomas, grasping the reason, also hared home, rejoicing that Mairi, likewise having been prevented by the weather from working in the hay, would probably not say no to an evening's fishing. The days were shortening rapidly but if he hurried there would still be time before it got too dark, he told himself. He was breathless with haste as he burst into the kitchen, the suggestion that they go fishing ready to leap from his tongue.

'Mum!' he began. But the woman who was bending over the range was not Mairi. Thomas stopped short, staring in consternation at the district nurse in her blue dress and white apron. He was used to seeing the nurse at the cottage. After she had paid her monthly visit to the school she usually called to have a cup of tea and a chat with Mairi. But now there were no cups or scones on the table and the nurse was in the act of moving a steaming kettle over to the hob. She turned and nodded at Thomas affirmatively as if he had asked a question.

'Your mother is not well,' she told him. 'She is away to her bed.'

The nurse's uniform coupled with her sharp voice brought back memories of an almost forgotten authority. 'Is Mum ill?' he asked timidly. In his mind there could be a big difference between being 'away to her bed' and being ill. He glanced at the bedroom door and then back again at the nurse.

'She's ill enough not to be bothered by anyone,' the nurse replied meaningly. 'Now drink this tea I've made for you and get yourself a piece of whatever you have with it. Then you'd best try and see what you can do to help.'

Thomas drank the tea obediently but there was a tightness somewhere in his stomach that blocked any desire for food. He went outside. It was too early to feed the hens but noticing that the peat pails had not been filled he carried them over to the peat shed.

When he returned with the full pails he asked the nurse, 'Is "himself" here?'

'Mr MacDonald is not here yet, no. I should think he will not be long. No doubt he will be getting a lift with the doctor when he comes.'

The doctor? Thomas experienced a cold tremor of fright. The doctor didn't come all the way out to Corrie unless there was something seriously wrong. He stood irresolutely by the door, wanting to ask more questions but, discouraged by the nurse's manner, he watched silently as she poured hot water from the kettle into a bowl, cooled it with water from the pail and then washed her hands. He was still watching her when they both heard footsteps outside.

'That will be the doctor and Mr MacDonald now,' said the nurse, drying her hands and preparing to follow the doctor into Mairi's room.

Thomas looked up. He had never seen 'himself' look so stonily grim-faced as when he entered the kitchen. Just looking at him brought back so much of his earlier fear that he could not stop himself from trembling. Sandy looked through him and, turning his back, stood staring out of the window, not moving until the nurse came out of Mairi's room.

'Away to your room for a wee whiley till I have a word with Mr MacDonald,' the nurse commanded Thomas. Reluctantly he went towards the passage but with his hand on the doorknob he paused and looked back. 'Himself'

had turned to face the nurse and the way the nurse
was looking up at him without speaking made Thomas
wonder if she too found 'himself' frightening. Catching
sight of Thomas still lingering by the door, she gestured
him impatiently away. Thomas closed the door behind
him and went slowly through to his own room. He heard
the doctor leave and assumed the nurse had also left but,
on his way out through the kitchen, he noticed her outdoor
clothes were still draped over a chair and wondered
fretfully how much longer she was going to stay? How
much longer she intended to keep him away from his
mum?

When he had seen to the hens he looked around for
other jobs to do. He built up the fire and refilled the kettle;
scrubbed the potatoes for their meal and set them on the
fire. He lit the lamp and prepared Ben's meal and last of
all he put 'himself's' slippers beside his chair. He was
sitting beside the fire when 'himself' came back into the
kitchen. Thomas waited tensely.

'You can go through now, boy,' he said. Thomas
jumped up but the nurse was there in the doorway ready
to restrain him.

'Now you must be very quiet and sit still. Mr Mac-
Donald is seeing me to my car so you're in charge, but only
until he gets back. Don't forget now,' she bade him. Torch
in hand she followed Sandy out into the darkness.

Very gently Thomas opened the door of Mairi's bedroom. The lamp had been turned low but he could see her
lying back against the pillows.

'Mum!' he called softly.

'Thomas!' Thomas had to check himself from rushing
towards the bed so relieved was he to hear her speak. As he
drew closer he saw she was smiling at him and holding out
her hands. When he bent over her, she cupped his face in
her hands tenderly. 'Oh, Thomas, did you get a fright

coming home and finding me in bed?' she asked. 'Oh, I'm sorry,' she added seeing his miserable expression.

'Are you feeling b-better now, Mum?'

'Lots better,' she told him. 'I'll be perfectly all right soon but the doctor says I'm to go into hospital for a few days just to make sure I have a good rest,' she added.

'Hospital?' There was panic in Thomas's voice.

'Just for a few days. It's silly really but the doctor thinks I won't get proper rest if I stay here.' She put a finger under his chin. 'Don't look so glum about it,' she said.

'It was awful coming home and you not there smiling at me.' His teeth were pulling at his bottom lip and in the lamplight his eyes were shiny with tears. 'If I had to go from here I'd miss your smile more than anything else in the world,' he told her.

'Oh, Thomas,' she said, her eyes caressing him.

They talked quietly until Sandy came back and said the nurse's instructions were that her patient must now settle down for the night. Thomas made no attempt to prolong his time in the bedroom because, even while they had been talking to each other, he had noticed her eyelids fluttering as if sleep had begun to press them down.

The nurse was back at the cottage when Thomas woke up the next morning. 'Get your breakfast and make yourself useful as you can,' she told Thomas. 'There's plenty to do.' She bustled back to the bedroom.

Thomas, resenting her tone and the implication that he would not be making himself useful, went sulkily about his morning tasks. The next time he saw her he said, 'Can I go in to see Mum before I go to school?'

The nurse's voice lost its sharpness. 'Aye, you can do that, laddie. She's been looking for you to go already.'

She was sitting up when the nurse ushered him into the bedroom and in the daylight Thomas thought she looked strangely pale and tired. But she had not lost her smile.

'Thomas,' she said, indicating the chest of drawers which stood beneath the window, 'in that top drawer you will find a thin flat cardboard box. Will you get it and bring it to me, please?' He found the box and took it to her and when she opened it he saw it was a box neatly packed with embroidered handkerchiefs.

'This was a present from my husband for my birthday,' she told Thomas. 'I haven't used one of them yet but I will be taking them to hospital when I go so I shall have something pretty to wipe my nose on in front of all the other patients.' She chuckled faintly. 'But this one,' she took out one of the handkerchiefs and unfolded it. 'This one is for you and d'you know what I'm going to do with it first?' Thomas gave her a puzzled smile. 'You remember you said you'd miss something more than anything in the world?' Thomas nodded. 'Well, I'm going to wrap one of my smiles in this for you to keep while I'm away.' She held the handkerchief over her face and above it her eyes glinted with fun. 'There!' She folded it quickly back into shape and put it into his hand. 'Keep it safe and don't waste it,' she cautioned. They grinned at each other intimately.

The nurse opened the door. 'Time's up,' she announced. 'And it's past time you were on your way to school, laddie,' she added.

He wanted to ask his mum if it wouldn't be wiser for him to stay at home but something told him he must not bother her with questions which needed a decisive answer. He knew he ought to ask 'himself', but 'himself', the nurse told Thomas, was up on the croft keeping a lookout for the ambulance. Thomas went dolefully to school.

8

The thought of his mum in hospital had been pressing heavily on Thomas's mind all day, and after school the sight of a disconsolate Ben emphasized the fact that she would not be there to greet him when he entered the kitchen.

Mrs McAlister, Shamus's mother, stood in the doorway. 'You will be staying with myself and Shamus while

Mairi is away in hospital,' she told Thomas. 'Sandy will likely stay by her a good part of the time so he says for you to see to Ben.'

Thomas gaped at her. 'I don't need to stay anywhere but here,' he protested. 'Mum taught me how to cook and I'd sooner sleep here. I'll be all right with Ben for company.' Mrs McAlister was looking at him shrewdly. 'I want to stay here, truly. I can do most of the jobs myself now.'

Mrs McAlister was in some way relieved though she did not show it. 'You will come for your evening meal,' she insisted serenely. 'For the rest, I dare say you're as well able to look after yourself as any other body that's lived on a croft. Very well, I will tell that to Sandy myself when I see him next.'

Ben, obviously lost without his master, followed Thomas to school next morning and was there waiting for him outside the school in the evening. It was the same the next day. He slept in Thomas's bedroom at night and when the weekend came the boy and the dog were inseparable. Thomas carried on with as much work as he could around the croft, leaving the cottage only to go to school and to Mrs McAlister's for a meal. He didn't think much of Mrs McAlister's cooking, but Mr McAlister, who was keeping an eye on everything during Sandy's absence, went up to the post office every day to telephone through for news of Mairi. The news he was given did not greatly increase Thomas's worry. She was still tired was all Mr McAlister told him; she still needed rest.

'Tell her to get better as quickly as she can and tell her I'm managing fine by myself,' he said to Mr McAlister, though there was a note of wistful uncertainty in his voice. But when, after a day or two there was still no news of her coming home, he asked Mrs McAlister, 'If she's not coming home soon, d'you think they'll let me go and see her?'

'Indeed, I'm sure they'll do just that,' replied Mrs McAlister. 'Maybe in a day or two.'

The following day was the start of the half-term holiday, so Thomas was at home getting on with his self-appointed chores. He was in the peat shed, the door propped open to give some light while he filled the peat pails, when Ben started to bark suddenly. Thomas heard a strident female voice and looking out saw an enormously fat tinker woman with her almost equally enormous bundle slung over her shoulder. She was standing in a rather proprietary way in front of the open door of the cottage.

'Where is the lady of the house?' she demanded to know.

'She is away from home,' Thomas called back mistrustfully.

'Oh, my! Then is there not a body here that would be wanting to see the fine things I have in my pack?' she responded plaintively. 'What about yourself, now? Would not a young man such as yourself be wanting a wee thing for his mother or his sister?' She set her pack down in the doorway and began untying it.

Thomas was for a moment troubled by her persistency but then a thought came to him. It would be his mum's birthday the following Thursday and for weeks, in the hope of being able to get across to the mainland to buy her a present, he had been saving up his pocket money. He knew there was no likelihood of making such a trip while she was in hospital, so approaching the tinker he asked hesitantly if there were any aprons in her bundle. 'P-pretty c-coloured ones, I mean,' he stressed.

'Indeed I have so,' the woman assured him, juggling through the contents of her bundle and offering several aprons for inspection. Thomas thought them all inexpressibly drab, as indeed appeared to be everything else she offered. He shook his head but the tinker woman

85

doubled her persuasion, tipping up the whole bundle in her enthusiasm. Glimpsing an edge of colour among the pile, Thomas pointed to it.

'What's that?' he asked.

With a flourish the woman extracted and held up a tablecloth, stretching her arms wide to display it fully. The cloth was bright yellow with a deep blue border and a centrepiece of red flowers. Thomas knew it was exactly right. The bargain was completed and the tinker woman departed. Thomas, taking the cloth through to his bedroom, hid it in a drawer and for the rest of the day went about his work more cheerfully than he had since Mairi had gone to hospital.

Two days later when he was at the McAlisters' he had a message that he was to catch the bus next morning and go to the hospital. So she was getting better at last! Thomas felt an overwhelming sense of relief. Tomorrow would be Wednesday and he debated with himself whether or not he should take the tablecloth with him so she would have it to look at on her birthday the next day, but he decided against it. Much better now to wait until she arrived home and then spread the new cloth on the table all ready for her.

A woman he had never met before was waiting by the bus stop.

'You will be the Corrie laddie?' she greeted him. She took him to the hospital and as they entered she bade him fussily, 'Quiet now. Don't make a noise.'

The warning was scarcely necessary. Thomas was too subdued by the smell and the orderliness of the hospital even to whisper.

A door opened and a nurse came out of one of the rooms along the corridor. The woman urged Thomas forward and then left. As the nurse stood aside to let him enter the room, Thomas was aware of 'himself' sitting in a chair between the bed and the window. Thomas tiptoed across the room, coming to a stricken halt beside the bed with his eyes fixed on the face, so thin it could have been that of a stranger; so pale had it not been for the frame of golden hair it would have merged into the whiteness of the pillow.

Thomas saw 'himself' bend over the bed. 'It's the boy come to see you, Mairi. Thomas.' He indicated to Thomas that he should come closer.

'Hello, Mum!' Thomas's voice seemed to tie itself into such a tight knot that even he thought his greeting must have been barely distinguishable. But he saw the eyelids lift fractionally, giving him a fleeting glimpse of grey before they fluttered and closed again. The fingers of the strangely thin hand on the counterpane flexed weakly and though Thomas longed to touch her he was loath to do so for fear his own hand, now so rough in contrast, might chafe the paper-thin skin.

'Mum!' he whispered again. 'Mum!' he pleaded, his eyes searching for some further sign that she heard him. The eyelids fluttered again and he thought he heard her give a faint sigh.

It seemed to Thomas less than a minute before the nurse was back and touching him lightly on the shoulder. 'Say goodbye, now,' she said. 'We mustn't tire her any more.'

He looked helplessly at Sandy but Sandy was looking at his wife. He had to kneel on a chair to reach over and kiss her pale cheeks and as his lips touched her he was swept by the frightening conviction that his mum had already gone too far away to respond to him; too far ever to return. As the nurse led him out of the room he turned to look back, but 'himself' was still bending over the bed so he could not see the mingled anguish and entreaty in the glance Thomas directed at him.

He followed the nurse along the shiny, bare hospital

corridor and with every step the certainty that his mum was going to be taken away from him for ever, just as his granny had been taken away, seemed to rise up and strike him. It bore pitilessly into his mind, making him clench his jaws to stop them trembling. And then anger came; a smouldering deep-down anger that in some way helped to neutralize the soreness of grief. He was angry with the doctor who had sent her to hospital; angry with the hospital for not making her better; angry with God and Jesus and Heaven and the angels. But he let no one detect his anger, hiding it from the nurses who tried to be kind; hiding it from the white-coated doctors who did not try to be anything. It was with him as he walked beside yet another stranger who had been deputed to see him on the bus; it enclosed him as the bus jogged its way back along the Corrie road; and even when he found Mr McAlister had brought Ben to meet him at the end of the journey, his anger abated only enough for him to give them a stilted greeting.

Mr McAlister stayed late that night. How late Thomas did not know because he himself went to bed early, taking his anger with him and nursing it until it was temporarily swamped by tears. But the next morning he rescued his anger to use it like a bandage over his hurt so it would not be so easily discernible.

When he was at the McAlisters' the next day they told him with what he knew was false cheerfulness that the news was a little better that morning. But again, when evening came, Mr McAlister called and stayed late, and Thomas, finding his presence strangely comforting, went early to bed. He had lain awake for a long time staring at the ceiling which in the lamplight alternately gleamed and dulled as fragments of feebly nourished hope chased great clods of despair through his mind. It seemed to him he had been asleep only for a few minutes when he was wakened by Ben's whining and the sound of footsteps outside; slow heavy footsteps which did not sound at all like 'himself's' footsteps though Thomas knew, from Ben's excited reaction, that it could be no one else. He heard the low disjointed mumble of talk in the kitchen. He heard Mr McAlister depart without any called farewell. And as he lit the lamp he knew with a final dreadful certainty that his mum was dead.

With uneasy yearning he allowed himself to wonder if, on seeing the light, 'himself' might come to his bedroom and share the terrible news with him, but though he listened intently there came no further sound from the kitchen; no footsteps in the passageway.

From the moment he had heard his master return, Ben had been snuffling along the bottom of the door of the bedroom, whining imploringly and scratching. Thomas got up and opened the door. The kitchen door was closed but Ben ran to it and whined again more urgently. Thomas hesitated. There was a rim of light showing beneath the door so, surely, if 'himself' was in the room, he would hear Ben and let him through? But though Ben's scratching became more persistent there was no sound of movement. Thomas forced himself to go forward and gingerly open the door.

Sandy, still wearing his outdoor clothes, was sitting in his chair beside the cold range, staring bleakly into space. Only when Ben pushed his attention on him did he stir and look across at Thomas who was standing mutely still, holding the doorhandle and shivering with cold and dread. Sandy's gaze shifted from him and for a few moments he did not speak. Then in a flat, distant voice he said, 'She is gone.' Thomas made no sound or movement. Hearing the words spoken seemed to him to wound even deeper than the knowledge. 'She is dead, d'you hear me?' Sandy's voice was now harsh and thick. Except for the dry sobs that heaved at his chest Thomas still did not move. Sandy brushed a hand across his brow. 'Go, try and get some sleep, boy,' he bade, striving to soften his voice, but the need to be alone was so overpowering that when Thomas made no move to go his tone became peremptory. 'Go now.' As if he had been struck, Thomas closed the door and rushed blindly to his bedroom.

The faintly familiar smell of burning wick made him realize his lamp must be running dry and he turned it out and lay down, pulling the bedclothes around him. Not welcoming sleep, he stared into the darkness, shivering still even beneath the bedclothes. Without Mairi what was going to happen to him? He moaned into his pillow and the anger that had throbbed inside him since his visit to the hospital slowly drained away; the sharpness of his grief became blunted and as the cold gradually released its grip on his body he was conscious only of a feeling of utter desolation.

9

Thomas woke to the white light of snow reflected from the thinly clad hills and, in the misty seconds before the ache of sorrow reasserted itself, his mind ran through the routine he had established while he had been coping alone. Rekindle the fire; make the porridge; milk the cow and put her out to graze; feed the hens. . . . No doubt now 'himself' was home he would be taking over some of the morning work but, for today at any rate, Thomas was

91

eager to carry on as he had been. Entering the kitchen, he was disconcerted to see the fire already brightly ablaze and the porridge pan keeping warm on the hob. Going into the larder to get the milking pail he found the pail already full of fresh milk. 'Himself' must have got up early and done the chores, Thomas realized. But where was he now? He listened for noises that would indicate that 'himself' was still busy about the cottage, but hearing none, he wondered if he had gone back to bed. But no, for then Ben would have been left in the kitchen and there was no sign of Ben anywhere. Had 'himself' already gone off to the hill or out to his creels, leaving him alone? Slowly the awesome silence of the room closed in on him. He had been on his own here much of the time Mairi had been in hospital without being afraid, but now, though death had not entered the cottage, the pervasiveness of death pressed all around him. Trying to brace himself against mounting trepidation, he rushed to the door and stood there staring at the sleety rain while telling himself that to be afraid in the cottage now was almost like being a traitor to Mairi. But his mind refused to accept that the unnerving silence of the kitchen was in any way connected with Mairi. It was the aura of death that was frightening and to Thomas death seemed an entirely separate and daunting thing. His glance strayed to the henhouse and with a spark of relief he saw that the hens had not yet been let out and fed. As he poured corn into a bowl to take to them he recognized with relief that the aura of death in the cottage was not solely responsible for his uneasiness; a portion of it had been caused by the despairing suspicion that 'himself', having resolved to send him back to the orphanage, was intending to lose no time in assuming responsibility for all the work of the croft, including that of feeding the hens which for so long now Thomas had come to regard as a task that was his alone.

He had no appetite for breakfast but, because Mairi would have urged him to do so, he ladled porridge into a bowl, sluiced it with milk and ate it, standing by the open door rather than in the kitchen. He wished fervently for 'himself' to appear. 'Himself' would bring his own silence but his presence there would leave no room for ghosts.

He considered what he should do with his day. Whether or not he should go to school; whether he dared go to school for though he now felt emptied of weeping he was uncertain if he could trust himself not to break down in front of the other children. His mind switched to wondering about 'himself'; whether, when he came back to the cottage, he would expect to find Thomas there; whether, on the other hand, 'himself' would be cross if he found he had absented himself from school. Had the day been less discouraging, he would have chosen to go down to the shore and there, safe in his regular hideout, try calling to the seals, which had now returned to frequent the bay, and, in the belief that they would bring him comfort, tell them the extent of his wretchedness. But the day was sleety and cold and the rapidly rising wind, which had already churned the waters of the bay too fiercely for any seal to be visible from the shore, would, with the flowing tide, soon be sending lashings of spray to flood every nook and cranny of the rocks.

Unable to thrust down his fear of being alone in the cottage, Thomas set out for school, his feet growing more leaden with every step he took. Once there, the unspoken compassion of his schoolmates came near to tearing down the flimsy shutters with which he had tried to cover his heartache and he longed for the time of release. Shamus whispered a message that the arrangement for him to take his meals with the family was to continue for the time being and that until after the funeral was over he was also to sleep there. Thomas did not demur. The memory of losing his granny had almost vanished from his mind, but he had seen Corrie's dreary and neglected burial ground and the thought of Mairi being lowered into a wet, dark hole and left there was like a physical pain, and he was grateful that there was to be a friendly place to which he could withdraw until it was all over.

Though he suspected that without Mairi the cottage would be little more than a hollow replica of the home he had known, he still felt possessive about it and was eager to return to it. He could think of no other place where he belonged more, but in the meantime he was relieved to submit himself to the kindly supervision of the McAlisters who were companionable rather than tight-lipped and whose home was quiet rather than silent.

He did not forsake the cottage while he was with the McAlisters but trekked twice daily across the stretch of moor that divided the two crofts to feed and water the hens. At first he had worried lest he should arrive to find them already attended to, but as if by tacit agreement 'himself' continued to leave the task for Thomas. While he was there he made himself go into the cottage and check that the water pails were full and that there was dry peats for the fire ready for when 'himself' came home of an evening, but he never stayed longer than was necessary for him to carry out his tasks. Although he could not identify in his mind the recent ghosts, they seemed to have claimed possession of the cottage, making him recoil from being there alone. It would be different when 'himself' was there too, he thought. There would be memories then but no ghosts, and even if he and 'himself' were unable to communicate sufficiently to share the memories, their love for Mairi must surely bring them to some sort of alliance. Thomas buoyed up his hopes by recalling how, when they had worked together to rescue the young seal, they had seemed to teeter on the edge of an unspoken understanding. Recognizing that they each, for different reasons, suffered from a lack of communicativeness, he wondered if, now they were to be on their own in the cottage, they might at some time achieve a kind of dour companionship.

The day following the funeral Thomas was fully expecting to be told he would now be returning to live in the cottage, but when he asked Mrs McAlister she appeared to become a little embarrassed. 'Give it a day or two yet, laddie,' she told him. The awful suspicion that 'himself' did not want him back at the cottage, that now Mairi was dead he was to be sent back to the orphanage without having the chance to plead to be allowed to stay, began to plague Thomas. He began to fear that the adoption papers might never be signed. He tried sounding Mrs McAlister as to whether 'himself' had spoken of any plans for his future.

'No, indeed. But hasn't the poor man enough to worry him. But he's a good, kind man and you can be sure whatever he decides it will be because he believes it will be the best for you.' She shook her head sadly.

Thomas was in no way reassured by her reply. 'Mum would have wanted him to keep me here,' he claimed.

'Aye, indeed,' Mrs McAlister agreed.

Three days passed. Three days and nights of miserable conjecture for Thomas as suspicion became conviction. And then on the fourth evening when he was trying to concentrate on playing a game of cards with Shamus he heard Mrs McAlister blandly telling her husband that she would be going over to the cottage the next morning to help get it 'sorted' ready for Thomas's return. A throb of relief lightened his gloom and for a moment there was a mist in front of his eyes so he could not see the cards. So he was to return! He was concerned as to why the cottage had to be 'sorted' before he could return to it but his main concern was to get back and immediately become so involved in the work of the croft that 'himself' would come to think of him as being indispensable.

It was not until Mrs McAlister was in the midst of preparations for their meal the next evening that she calmly informed Thomas he was to return to the cottage as soon as the meal was over. Thomas caught his breath. Now that the time had come he found he was neither elated nor cast down by the news. It was not going to be the same going back with no Mairi calling out her cheery greeting; her voice trilled through his memory: 'There's yourself now, is it, Thomas?' And on she would go, telling him of incidents that had happened during the day or questioning him about his own day. All the time she had been in hospital he had been saving up things to tell her, but who would want to hear them now? Not 'himself'. Even if 'himself' decided to let him remain at Corrie, Thomas doubted if their relationship would progress far enough for 'himself' to pretend an interest in him.

Mr McAlister came in, stamping his feet in the doorway. 'My, but that last shower has brought the dark almost on top of us,' he commented.

Thomas glanced at the uncurtained window, opaque now against the gathering darkness. By the time they had eaten their meal the night would be pitch black. Getting up, he went to the door and looked anxiously at the sky, willing the daylight to drag its feet until he could get back. He considered telling Mrs McAlister he was feeling unwell and didn't want anything to eat so he could set out right away and reach the cottage before it got too dark, but he guessed she would find some reason for not allowing him to rush off so quickly. He closed the door and sat down again, though his glance went again and again from the blackening square of the window to the range where Mrs McAlister was shuffling cooking pots about. Frantically his mind urged her to hurry. At last the food was ready. He gulped it down.

'There now, Thomas. Seeing you will be back sleeping in your own bed tonight, you should gather up what you have to take with you, now,' Mrs McAlister said when the meal was over.

With his bag under his arm Thomas asked diffidently, 'C-can I b-borrow a lantern?' His stammer returned as his agitation increased.

Mr McAlister got up from his chair and looked outside but any hopes that Thomas may have had that he would offer to accompany him were quickly dashed. 'There's a good half of a moon up there will give you more light than a lantern,' he said.

Thomas fidgeted around, taking out and then replacing the contents of his bag, the urge to plead to be escorted warring with the shame he would feel at having to do so. He gritted his teeth. He must find the courage to go alone.

He picked up his bag and at the same moment there came the sound of a foot scraping against the step outside. The door opened and 'himself' stood in the doorway with Ben at his heels.

'So there you are,' Mrs McAlister greeted him as if she had been expecting him. 'And here's Thomas been waiting for you for this past half hour just,' she added.

Sagging with relief, Thomas looked up at him. It was the first time he had seen 'himself' since the night Mairi died. One small tear formed in the corner of each eye as he recalled the scene.

'Aye, well, Thomas. If you're ready, we'll be getting ourselves back now.' His tone sounded more lenient, more gentle than Thomas had ever heard it.

'Surely you will stay and take a wee strupak with us now you're here?' coaxed Mrs McAlister.

'No, indeed. We'd best get back. There's a good frost

on, I'm thinking, and the longer we leave it the worse the going will be.' He turned and opened the door. 'Are you ready, Thomas?'

As he walked confidently beside 'himself' over the crisp heather, the moon shadows which would have pursued Thomas had he been on his own now held no menace. A comforting sensation of warmth began to seep through his body, combating not just the coldness of the night but driving out the chill of fear which had been steadily building up inside him for the past hour or more.

The cottage window, aglow with lamplight, was so expected and familiar that, in a moment of fantasy, Thomas bounded forward. An instant later he had recovered himself. She wouldn't be there. 'Himself' must have lit the lamp before he had come to meet him. The moment lacerated him and as he opened the door the knowledge that she would never be there again seemed to rush at him, making him cower back. 'Himself' was close behind him.

'Well, Thomas,' he said. 'Likely you could do with a cup of tea to warm you after being out in the cold.' He swung the kettle over the fire. Thomas noticed 'himself' did not take tea but instead got out the whisky bottle and a glass which he filled to the brim.

'G-good night!' Thomas said when he had finished his tea. He got a nod in reply.

Before he got into bed he took out the handkerchief Mairi had given him and put it under his pillow.

10

Gusts of wind were thumping against the corner of the
house; rain and hail were rattling against the bedroom
window, and to Thomas the morning seemed to be even
darker than the night had been. Lighting the candle, he
dressed quickly and went through the still, dark kitchen
where, reassuringly, Ben stirred and came to greet him.
He lit the lamp and, with the intention of having breakfast

99

all prepared for when 'himself' appeared, hurriedly laid dry peats among the hot embers of the fire and, with the bellows, blew them into a blaze.

While the porridge was cooking he went to get a table-cloth from the drawer in the dresser. With a slight start he drew back as his hand found only emptiness. Surmising that Mrs McAlister must have moved the tablecloths to a different drawer during her 'sorting' at the cottage, he opened another drawer, and then another. There were no tablecloths in any of them. Troubled by their disappearance and with mounting resentment against Mrs McAlister for interfering with the way things had always been, he opened cupboard after cupboard seeking the tablecloths among the crockery and the food stores, but without result. The thought struck him suddenly that Mairi had kept her clean aprons in one of the dresser drawers and yet he had seen no aprons either. With growing uneasiness he let his eyes travel slowly around the kitchen looking for other signs of change.

When he had arrived at the cottage with 'himself' the previous evening one change had forced itself upon his attention, that being that Mairi's chair which, during the day, was usually pushed back against the wall so as to allow for easier access to the range, had not been pulled up to the fire opposite 'himself's' chair as was customary in the evenings. The empty space where he had expected her chair to be so sharply emphasized her absence that Thomas had tried to keep his eyes averted from that corner of the room, so he had missed seeing then what he was seeing all too plainly now, that her workbag in which she had kept her knitting and her spectacles, and which had always hung from the arm of her chair as if its handle had taken root, was no longer there. He moved over to the chair, running his hands tremulously along the arms as if it were Mairi herself he was touching. As he turned away yet another implication of death scratched remorselessly at his mind.

He set two porridge bowls and two mugs on the bare table and, when the porridge was ready, ladled a portion into his own bowl. Mairi had always insisted that porridge in a morning gave people strength to face the day, so he managed to eat a few spoonfuls. So far there had been no sound of movement from the other bedroom and, since the morning was growing lighter, Thomas put on his oilskins and gumboots and went out to feed the hens and milk the cow. 'Himself' was putting on oilskins ready to go outside when Thomas returned.

'There was no need for that,' he said, glancing at the full milk pail. 'I will myself see to the milking.' The flat firm voice brooked no contradiction, but Thomas surprised himself by finding his own voice.

'I c-can d-do it. I'd like t-to,' he argued timidly.

'You can get yourself away to school. I am away myself now but I will be back before dark.' The tone was still unyielding, but Thomas's lurking fear that he might be left alone there at night was allayed. He carried the milk pail into the larder and as he was pouring it into the setting bowls he heard 'himself' whistle Ben and the door closing behind them. When he returned to the kitchen he was disappointed to see the other porridge bowl and mug had not been used. He washed his own breakfast dishes, leaving the others in case 'himself' came back and then he sat for a few minutes in 'himself's' chair, his hands gripping the wooden arms and the tears squeezing under his eyelids as he wondered what it was like to be big and strong and seemingly little affected by death.

His thoughts returned to the missing tablecloths and aprons and, curious to know what had happened to them, he plucked up courage to go into the other bedroom. Opening the door cautiously, as if he suspected he might be confronted by some presence, he stepped inside, catching his breath as he saw the rumpled, unmade bed, bare now of the valance and coloured bedspread he remembered. The chest of drawers, the top of which had served Mairi as a dressing table, was also bare, as was the top of the bedside chest where there had stood a framed photograph of herself and 'himself' on their wedding day. Thomas stared and the bareness seemed to stare back at him as if proclaiming the end of Mairi's occupancy. He had intended peeping into the drawers to see if the tablecloths and aprons were hidden away there, but the cold colourlessness of the room unnerved him, making him loath to touch anything. Closing the door quietly, he returned to the kitchen where he made himself a lunch 'piecey' before getting into his oilskins again ready to go to school.

When he came home from school Ben was waiting to greet him so Thomas knew 'himself' could not be far away. Eager to please, he got some potatoes from the shed and was scrubbing them ready for the cooking pot when 'himself' returned carrying the full milk pail.

'You can feed that to the hens,' he told Thomas, nodding towards the pail.

Thomas did not feed the milk to the hens. Instead he took it to the larder where, again, he poured it into setting bowls with the intention of proving his usefulness by skimming it to make butter as Mairi had taught him. After he had finished his outside chores he put the pan of potatoes on the fire to cook while he looked in the larder for fish or meat. His eye was caught by two freshly skinned and paunched rabbits which hung from a hook near the window. On the stone shelf beside them stood a plate of fresh filleted fish. Thomas preferred the fish but hearing 'himself' moving in the kitchen he took down one of the rabbits and carrying the rabbit in one hand and the plate of fish in the other he proffered them inquiringly.

'Anything you've a mind for, boy,' Sandy snapped, and turned away as if irritated by the sight of food.

Undeterred, Thomas carried on preparing a meal sufficient for the two of them, but to his dismay when it was ready 'himself' disappeared into his bedroom where he stayed until after Thomas had gone to bed.

It was the same the next day and the next, but still Thomas refused to be discouraged. Each morning he got up in time to cook the porridge and when he came home from school he started to prepare the evening meal. 'Himself' seemed to accept that despite his age Thomas had learned to cook well enough and there was always meat or fish in the larder, but he never showed any inclination to join Thomas at the table nor indeed to show any interest in food. Thomas began to doubt whether 'himself' ate anything at all. He never saw him eat breakfast, but he reasoned that 'himself' must have eaten after he had left for school because when he came home from school the pan and dishes were always clean and back in their places. However, when the weekend came and he made the porridge as usual and, as usual, left it on the hob, he found it still there hours later, the smooth surface of the thickened meal undisturbed by the imprint of a ladle. Eventually he tipped it into the hen pail to be mixed with the mash and if 'himself' noticed it he made no comment.

It was much the same in the evenings. When the meal was ready, 'himself' always declined it, muttering something about eating later. But when morning came, though the pan and the dishes would have been washed and put away, more often than not when Thomas went to mix the hen mash he would find 'himself's' share of the meal he had cooked in the hen pail.

Where and what and when 'himself' ate became for Thomas a matter of increasing puzzlement. He wondered if he was buying food from the weekly grocery van and taking it to eat alone in some secret place such as the shepherd's bothy away up in the hills. He wondered if his cooking was spurned because it tasted less good than Mairi's cooking, and then again he wondered a little forlornly if 'himself' so strongly disapproved of his own presence in the cottage that any food he cooked had to be rejected.

Thomas wished fervently that he could speak of his worries, but 'himself''s reserve allowed neither comment nor question. The fact that he was not left alone in the cottage at night was a source of comfort to Thomas, but though they shared a kitchen there was no companionship between them. Evening after evening 'himself' either went to his bedroom or else sat in his chair with a book held in front of him but looking so stiff that it seemed as if he was adopting an attitude rather than reading. Thomas sat in his chair trying to read or to concentrate on some school work, but a strained silence separated them, pressing on Thomas his yearning for Mairi until his stretched nerves came near to goading him into shouted protestation. All too soon he would become aware of a growing restlessness and, apprehensive that it might bring a rebuke from 'himself', he would say goodnight and go to his room where, snugged up in bed against the cold, he would either read or make candle pictures the way Mairi had shown him.

Thomas was in no doubt that 'himself' was eager enough for him to say good night and go to bed. Indeed, his relief was almost as palpable as a firm push on the door closing behind him. He had little doubt as to the reason for it.

Except for the first evening back at the cottage after Mairi's death, 'himself' had avoided drinking in Thomas's presence, but Thomas knew only too well from the smell of whisky lingering in the kitchen when he got up in the morning that the abstinence ceased as soon as he had left the kitchen. The knowledge distressed him, adding to his worries. At the orphanage he had heard many tales of children being abandoned by drunken parents, even ill-treated by them, but though he had no fear that 'himself' would ever hurt him physically he did have a recurring fear that in a moment of drunken indifference he might temporarily forget how useful Thomas had become and might make an irreversible decision to send him back to the orphanage.

The extra work he had taken on gave Thomas little time for brooding during the day, but at night when he was in bed despondency sometimes ensnared him like a net from which he had to struggle to escape. Then he would convince himself that he had detected signs of preparations to send him away from Corrie. Even to send him back to the orphanage. When he woke in the mornings the weight of his imaginings would still be with him and all day he would be impatient for school to end so he could rush down to the shore and shout his fears to the seals. And after telling the seals, he would wander back up the croft thinking how terrible it would be if he had to leave Corrie and questioning how the hens and the cows would manage without him. If 'himself' was not in the byre he would go in there, letting his feet sink into the soft bedding of rushes as he talked to the cows and leaned on their warm gurgling bodies while they blew their strong breath over him. Oh, they were his! They were his! he cried silently. Had he not struggled to help harvest and carry the hay they were eating? Had he not helped to gather the rushes for their bedding? Surely no one would be cruel enough to part him from everything Mairi had taught him to help and to love? He felt that Corrie possessed him and he in turn felt possessive of everything that was Corrie. Not just the cottage and buildings, nor even the animals, but the croft and the crops it yielded; the hills, the burns, the lochs; the rain and the wind and the sea. So well he knew the different winds now and the way the sea shaped itself to meet them. If the door of the byre rattled, he knew the wind was westerly and the seas would be rolling towards the far shore and crashing against the point. If the hens hid themselves against the dyke, the wind had north in it and the breakers would be shorn so the spray plumed and raced along their length like the steam from an engine speeding through a deep cutting. The rain hitting his bedroom window meant it was driven by a southerly wind and the sea would be piling great breakers which reared and broke on the rocks immediately below the croft. When the wind whined around the house, the sea was mostly calm except for little frills of white that danced across the bay. All these things had inscribed themselves on his affections and he told himself he could never be happy away from them.

It was following upon one such spell of gloom, when he was wandering around the wilder parts of the croft half heartedly looking for traces of rabbit runs, that his eye was caught by a dark patch in a hollow that divided two outcrops of rock and, being familiar with every inch of the croft, he knew the patch had appeared since he was last there shortly before Mairi had died. Wondering if 'himself' had been working at something there, he went towards it. From the distance the ground looked as if there had been a fire there and he was puzzled because the regular place for burning rubbish was in a cleft of rock down by the shore. Closer investigation showed it to be a sodden pile of ash and charred shreds of material and, assuming that some tinkers must have stopped by and burned some of their rubbish where the fire would be screened from the cottage, he kicked distastefully at the pile. The next moment he was down on his knees, staring horror-stricken at what his foot had uncovered. The spectacles lay half buried among the ashes and though the lenses had gone and the metal frames were distorted Thomas recognized them beyond all doubt. They were Mairi's – his mum's spectacles which she had always worn when doing close work. The poignancy of the discovery made him cry out sharply; his chest began to heave as if his breath was being punched out of him. His uncertain fingers probed among the ash and, retrieving what was left of the spectacles, he raced back to the cottage, too confused in his mind to know why he was doing so. As he reached the cobbled path, 'himself' appeared in the doorway of the house. He waited, his eyes expressionless, his mouth a thin, inflexible line. Thomas, speechless and panting for breath, came to a halt in front of him and almost without realizing what he was doing he held out the spectacles. As his eyes lifted to 'himself's' face and he saw the grimness freeze swiftly into a stony greyness like a cloud shadow passing over a frost-coated hillside, his hand dropped weakly to his side and he shuddered at what he had done.

'Take those back to where you got them and never interfere again.' There was such steel in 'himself's' voice that Thomas felt the words striking him like spear thrusts. With a stifled sob he turned and fled back up the croft where he reburied the spectacles under the ashes.

It did not occur to him for some time that the charred shreds of material he had seen could have been anything but the rags he had assumed them to be, but it came to him later that they might have been the remains of the missing tablecloths and aprons. The realization brought with it a desperate longing for communication and understanding. He resolved to confide in Mrs McAlister, telling her not only about the discovery of the spectacles and 'himself''s' reaction, but about his whisky drinking and also about his own suspicions that 'himself' was not eating anything at all.

She was sympathetic but she did not seem to be unduly perturbed. 'Aye, but a deep wound must be well cleaned before it can start to heal, laddie,' she said by way of explanation, and when she saw he only vaguely understood, she added, 'You will no doubt come to know these things better when you are a man yourself.'

Thomas tried to understand. He continued doing his best to help and make himself needed, but at no time was he rewarded by more than a distant nod of acknowledgement from 'himself'. The weeks went by and, there being no noticeable change in the relationship with 'himself', Thomas grew increasingly disconsolate. The winter was in full stride now; the weather at its most savage; the days at their shortest. It was only just light when he set off for school and nearly dusk before he got home at night. The hills were snow-cloaked, their whiteness cleft by narrow burns that raced to pour themselves into rivers that in turn hurled themselves into the sea. Icicles hung like sets of organ pipes from overhanging rocks while rushes stood like grey sentinels guarding the stillness of the frozen lochans.

Despite good fires in the range, a cold austerity which Thomas could do nothing to alleviate seemed to have settled over the kitchen of the cottage and he blamed it on the silence which had supplanted the laughter and talk there had been when Mairi was alive. He wished he was old enough to be more of a companion for 'himself' and the wish reminded him that he would soon be ten.

He recollected his last birthday and the cake Mairi had made and decorated for him. How quickly that had been eaten! How cosy the evening had been, with even 'himself' shedding enough of his reserve to comment on the darra

Mairi had given him for his birthday present. As his thoughts swung back a bold plan began to take shape in his head.

On his birthday Thomas hurried home from school so as to be at the cottage in plenty of time before 'himself' returned. As soon as he had the preparations for the meal well in hand, he went to the drawer where he had hidden the tablecloth he had bought from the tinker and which he had wanted to give Mairi for her birthday present. There had been no tablecloth on the table since Mairi's death and Thomas felt a little nervous as he spread the cloth now. In the centre of the table he placed a dish and on the dish he set a pink-iced cake which Mrs McAlister, at his request, had brought back from the mainland for him the day before. The cake hadn't the nice sweet smell of the one Mairi had baked for him and he had been unable to find any bog cotton to decorate it, but Thomas was pleased enough. He stepped back to admire it. The tablecloth seemed to bring Mairi's presence back into the kitchen and he had a warm feeling that she was near and approving of his plan. When he heard 'himself's' footsteps on the cobbles outside, the cautious optimism he had nursed since he first conceived the idea gradually gave way to doubt. Would 'himself' break his reserve now and wish him a happy birthday? Would he notice the birthday cake and the bright cloth and remember what a happy day it had been last year? Thomas felt his breath grow tight in his chest; his mouth gave a little quiver of anticipation. The door opened.

Sandy stood stiffly, staring at the table as if he could not believe his eyes. Suddenly the stiffness seemed to slacken and striding forward he grabbed at a corner of the cloth as if he was about to tear it off the table. Thomas, fearing for the safety of the cake, jumped up to rescue it, and as he stood clutching the plate, his eyes, dark with anguish and entreaty, were fixed on Sandy. Sandy's fingers released their grip of the cloth.

'You should keep that for yourself,' he said, tight-jawed. Picking up the milk pail, he went out to the byre. It was a long time before he came back and by then Thomas had taken the tablecloth back to his room and hidden it again in the drawer. He had managed to eat a few mouthfuls of food but he had not touched the cake. Brooding over the failure of his plan, he went early to bed and lay miserably trying to fathom why whatever he did seemed to displease 'himself'.

He slept fitfully and, waking with a dry throat, he lit his candle intending to get a drink of water from the kitchen. The lamp was still burning and Thomas could not decide whether he had not slept as long as he thought or whether he had overslept and 'himself' was already up and about. Stealthily Thomas opened the door. 'Himself' was sitting by the table, his head resting on his arms, and Thomas thought he was snoring. The whisky bottle and glass were beside him. Thomas crept to the water pail, helped himself to a drink and was creeping back when Ben thumped his tail on the floor and immediately 'himself' raised his head and looked at Thomas.

'I was thirsty,' Thomas mumbled as he hurried back to his room. But he was disturbed by what he had seen. The strange slackness of 'himself's' shoulders, the drooped head on the arms, the unguarded hopelessness of his expression when he had looked up were all so at odds with the severe, inflexible man of whom he was so much in awe. As he thought over it, Thomas slowly began to grasp how deeply 'himself' had felt the blow of Mairi's death. 'Himself' had loved Mairi for a long time whereas he, because he had known her only a short time, had loved her only for a short time. He could not accept that he loved her less but a new feeling of tenderness towards 'himself' began to work its way into his mind. With sudden resolution he got out of bed again and, convinced that what he was about to do would please Mairi, he reached under his pillow for the handkerchief she had given him and made his way to the kitchen. 'Himself's' head was back on his arms but Thomas hesitated only for a second before going up to the table and pulling at his sleeve.

'You c-can b-borrow this,' he said when Sandy looked up. 'She g-gave it to me. She wrapped one of her smiles in it for me to k-keep always.' 'Himself' was staring at the handkerchief as if stupefied. 'I put it under my pillow at night and she c-comes and smiles and talks me to sleep.' Thomas paused, and as he looked into the bloodshot eyes that were still staring at him stupidly, Thomas's eyes were soft with pity. 'She'll c-come and talk to you too,' he promised. It seemed to Thomas he was offering the hand-kerchief for a long time before 'himself' reached out a hand to receive it. As he placed the folded handkerchief in the waiting palm he saw the strong fingers flex. 'D-Don't crush it!' His voice was sharp with alarm. The fingers relaxed. Thomas waited only a moment or two before he backed away from the table and returned to his room.

After the door closed behind Thomas, Sandy continued to stare at the handkerchief. Even through the stupor of drink he was stung by recognition and, turning his hand, he let the handkerchief drop on the table and reached for the whisky bottle. After refilling his glass, he looked at it with a kind of dazed loathing. He was perfectly aware he had already drunk far too much. Striving for forgetfulness, he had drunk too much every evening since Mairi had died. He would have continued his drinking during the day had not Mairi charged him to look after the boy, and for her sake he had done his best, not drinking until after Thomas had gone to bed for fear of becoming negligent.

He filled his glass again and yet again and not until the

lamp ran out of paraffin did he think of going to bed. Picking up the near empty whisky bottle and glass, he lurched through to his bedroom where, after topping up his glass, he put both bottle and glass down on the bedside chest and flung himself onto the bed, but a minute or two later his unsteady hand, groping for the whisky, caught the glass, knocking it over and spilling the contents on the top of the chest. He swore as he heard the liquid dripping onto the floor. His hand was wet from contact with the top of the chest and he wiped it on the bedclothes before rolling over to lie face downwards in the dark, abandoning himself to the drunken sleep he expected to overtake him. But sleep did not come so easily. The memory of the pity in Thomas's eyes when he had offered him the handkerchief would not be banished. Why, when he had reacted so angrily to the sight of the tablecloth and the cake, had the boy responded with pity? Shame and remorse combined to fend off the oblivion he sought. Why? Why? Question after question surfaced above the sluggishness of his brain. What had it cost the boy to offer to share with him what was obviously his most cherished memento of Mairi? Surely he, who had reacted so angrily to the sight of the tablecloth and the cake, might have reacted even more strongly against the sight of the handkerchief? And yet the boy with pity in his eyes had taken that risk. Why? Could it be that he considered him worth the sacrifice? He, who had offered to share nothing? He, who had been so implacable in his own grief that he had ruthlessly disposed of all those things which reminded him too grievously of his wife's death? A feeling of guilt forging its way through the fog of his whisky-befuddled senses reminded him that he had left the handkerchief lying on the table. Whatever his sins, he was not callous enough to leave it there for the boy to find in the morning. Rising from the bed, he lurched back to the kitchen and, picking up the handkerchief, took it to his bedroom. Steadying himself beside the bed, he was about to put the handkerchief on the bedside chest when his brain cleared enough to remind him of the spilled whisky. It would not be right to put the handkerchief down without first wiping the chest dry and he had nothing with which he could wipe it. He looked about dazedly and then, because his eyes would not focus on any place more suitable, he put the handkerchief down beside his pillow and slumped back onto the bed. And sleep came at last – deep sleep, such as he had not known since Mairi's death.

11

During the two weeks before Thomas's birthday the weather had been wild and wet, making it impossible for 'himself' to go to his creels or to catch any fish. However, on the day following his birthday, which was a Saturday, Thomas woke to a cold, crisp morning and a sea so calm it looked as if someone had taken the trouble to polish it to smoothness. After two weeks on a daily diet of salt herring

Thomas was longing for a taste of fresh fish and, convinced that 'himself' would sleep later than usual following his heavy drinking bout of the previous night, he resolved, with great daring, that when he had fed the hens he would take his darra and row out in *Puffin* to try to catch some fish. Ben watched him go but made no attempt to follow him and Thomas, knowing the dog would not move more than a few yards from the house whilst his master was still inside, did not encourage him. He felt more than a prick of conscience as he dragged *Puffin* down the shore, but once in the dinghy with the oars grasped firmly in his hands, he felt only a quickening of confidence. Looking back at the cottage he saw no sign of movement. With any luck, he thought, he might have caught enough fish and be back home before 'himself' was awake. Perhaps then 'himself' would at last be pleased with something he had done.

Despite his excessive drinking of the previous night, Sandy slept only a little later than usual that morning. Calm always awakened him more easily than the noisiest of storms, but since his mind was more crowded with thoughts than it had been for some weeks, he lay for a time letting them rearrange themselves into a sequence he could accept. When he did get up he found he had not bothered to take off his clothes the night before and, with a slight feeling of embarrassment, instead of going into the kitchen where he expected Thomas would be, he went to the door of the house and stood looking out at the tranquil day. It occurred to him that the extra whisky he had drunk must have had some kind of restorative effect since he was aware of a significant lightening of his spirits which could not have been wholly attributable to the freshness of the rapidly brightening day. Going into the kitchen he saw the fire had not been lit; that the porridge pan was still on the shelf and, with a twinge of self-reproach, that the birthday cake was still untouched on the dresser. Assuming Thomas was making the most of not having to get up for school, Sandy lit the fire and made the porridge before going out to milk the cow. On his way to the byre he was surprised to see the hens already fed and out foraging around the croft. So, Thomas was already up, he reflected. After the milking was finished he went back to the house, expecting to see Thomas in the kitchen, but when there was no sign of him he opened the door to the passage and called out. There being no reply, he opened the door of the bedroom. With a kind of mental raising of the eyebrows, he thought that the fine morning had tempted Thomas out early perhaps to set or to inspect his snares. He had intended by way of return for Thomas's offer of the handkerchief to suggest he came out to the lobster creels with him, but if the boy was not back in time that would have to be the end of it. He was conscious of a strange tinge of regret.

While he carried on with the rest of the morning chores he realized he was keeping an eye open for Thomas. He was not worried but the thought of the boy was on his mind, prodding him into examining his own behaviour. To Sandy's way of thinking, he had never rejected Thomas. He had never envisaged, as Thomas had so much feared, returning him to the orphanage, although, because the boy intruded on the dreary solitude he had imposed upon himself since his wife's death, he had thought of sending him away to school. He would be doing the right thing for Thomas, he had told himself, and if they saw each other only during the holidays they would each be better able to come to terms with their grief. But the scene of last night had shaken Sandy. Slowly his mind grasped the fact that it was not separation from each other that he and Thomas needed.

Ben broke into his introspection with a yip of excitement such as he would have made had he seen a stranger approaching or had he heard or scented something that told him all was not well. Sandy's gaze shifted to scan the hillside, but seeing no sign of sheep bunching or being harried in any way, his eyes searched the croft. Again he perceived nothing unusual.

'What is it, Ben?'

Ben's ears were pricked as if he had heard something and he was looking in the direction of the sea. At Sandy's words he began to rear and prance while he yipped insistently.

'Go after it then!' Ben bounded away down the croft and Sandy, knowing now that something was amiss, strode after him. As they neared the shore and Sandy's eyes focused on the small dark shape that was being tossed about in the tide rip, his striding changed to a swift leaping and running. Dragging down *Beulah*, he pulled with swift strong strokes towards the mouth of the bay and as the boat drew closer to *Puffin* he saw that Thomas had only one oar with which he was desperately trying to turn the boat. When they were closing in, Sandy shipped an oar and as the gunwales of the two boats crashed together he leaned over and heaved Thomas into the *Beulah*. The next moment he had hold of *Puffin*'s rope and was towing the dinghy behind. Thomas sat shivering in the stern of the boat, watching 'himself' expertly working *Beulah* out of the tide rip. As soon as they reached calm water he expected to hear the cold, angry·reprimand he knew he deserved.

Beulah was scraping on the shingle of the shore before 'himself' spoke. 'Get you up to the house and get yourself warm and dry!' he commanded. Thomas slid a glance at his face. The flinty expression was as hard as he had ever seen it; the mouth was set firm as a trap.

'I wanted t-t-to see if I c-c-could c-catch us some f-fish,' Thomas stammered through chattering teeth.

'Get you up to the house. And run all the way!' 'himself' reiterated peremptorily. Thomas ran. Sandy paused for a moment to watch the small figure fleeing in the direction of the cottage and a hurried smile flitted across his grim face as if he had been unable to forbid it.

When Sandy got back to the house Thomas was sitting, wrapped in a blanket, beside the blazing fire. His eyes widened as he saw 'himself' put two fish on the table.

'I c-caught three.' Thomas's tone was faintly indignant.

'The gulls, likely, got the other when my back was turned,' 'himself' said. 'Which of us is going to cook them?' Thomas was too surprised to reply. He had been waiting for the backlash of 'himself''s' anger and when it did not come he felt uneasy. He looked blankly.

'Are you dressed and dry under that blanket?' Thomas nodded. 'Right, then I'll do the cooking and you can set out on the table whatever we'll need to eat them.'

Thomas threw off the blanket, took it back to his bed-room and returned to the kitchen.

'Have you ever heard of such things as wedding break-fasts, Thomas?' 'himself' asked.

'Yes.' Thomas looked puzzled.

'Aye, well boy, seeing we'll both be feeling a bit hungry, why don't we have a birthday breakfast?' 'Himself' turned away from the range to glance at Thomas. 'Por-ridge, fresh-caught fish and birthday cake. How about that?'

Thomas, hardly able to believe his ears, reached for dishes and cutlery from the dresser and began to set them on the table.

'Wait you now!' Surprised, Thomas turned to see 'him-self' regarding him with a kind of rueful quizzicalness. 'Haven't you forgotten something?' Thomas watched as Sandy spread his hands in an unmistakable gesture over the table. Thomas's eyebrows shot up in swiftly dawning comprehension. Sandy's eyebrows lifted fractionally in confirmation. As Thomas darted through to his bedroom to get Mairi's birthday present tablecloth, his face lit with smiles.

'Himself' did not wish him a happy birthday as Thomas thought he might and they ate their birthday breakfast along with slices of birthday cake in the silence they had grown accustomed to sharing, but afterwards 'himself' said a little gruffly, 'If you're thinking you're not getting a present for your birthday, you're wrong.'

'A present?' Thomas echoed.

'Aye. From me and Ben. Alistair Ruag's bitch has some puppies. Ben's the father of them. I've spoken to Alistair to keep one for you.' Lying did not come easily to Sandy and he would not look at Thomas. True enough Alistair's bitch had some puppies; true, Ben was the father; but it was not true that he had spoken to Alistair about keeping a puppy. He would do that immediately he left the house. There would be no difficulty in getting one of the puppies for Thomas.

The little breath of caution that always came to tighten Thomas's chest before he could allow himself to accept anything pleasurable prevented him from crying out in delight. 'A pup! Of my own!' he said incredulously.

'Himself' nodded. 'Aye, it'll be ready in a week or two but you can go up and see it any time you have a mind to.'

Sandy rose from the table and went into the bedroom. A moment later he was back in the kitchen. 'You'd best take care of this,' he said, placing the handkerchief carefully on the dresser. Thomas looked up at him as if on the point of asking a question, but 'himself's' expression was so inscrutable the impulse to do so died. He knew he would never ask the question but he knew, or thought he knew, that the sharing of the handkerchief had created some bond between them. He doubted if 'himself' would ever need or accept the loan of the handkerchief again, but if he ever did then Thomas would offer it gladly and the smile would still be there to work its magic.

'Thank you.' Thomas could do little more than breathe the words. 'Oh, and thank you for saving me this morning,' he remembered to add.

'You need more practice in a boat before you go out on your own,' 'himself' told him, and Thomas was relieved that there was only faint censure in his tone. 'I must away to the hill now but not for more than an hour or two. I was thinking you can come out to the creels when I get back. We might catch a fish or two while we're about it.'

Thomas fought down his elation. 'C-can I?'

'Aye. Be ready!'

Thomas became emboldened. 'If I'm to have a puppy, I wouldn't be able to take it with me if you sent me back to the orphanage,' he said.

'You want to go back?' Sandy shot him a quick glance.

'No.'

'Then you'll not go.'

The four words spoken so emphatically seemed to Thomas like being given four more birthday presents. 'Himself' was known as a man who kept his promises. From now on he could cast off all fear of being sent away from Corrie.

'There's just one thing,' Sandy said. 'I had a mind I might send you to a good school.' He saw Thomas's face fall. 'The schoolmistress says you have a good brain and it would be a pity to waste it.'

'I d-don't want to go away to school,' Thomas protested. 'I like being at the Corrie school.'

'Education's a grand thing, boy. You must think what you want to be when you're a grown man. A doctor, maybe, or a minister.'

'I want to be a crofter and work with sheep and fish lobster creels just like you,' Thomas stated flatly.

'Aye, well. I'll leave it to you to tell me if you change your mind. A partner in the boat would be a great help and an extra pair of legs on the hill never comes amiss.' Sandy spoke nonchalantly, but Thomas sat still, letting the thrill of this new relationship between them sink into his mind.

Had it come about as the result of what he was now seeing as his small adventure in *Puffin* that morning? Or hadn't it? His mind grew hazy trying to answer his own question and he gave up. All he knew was that, though there had been a change, he must accept that 'himself' would never change his manner. His dourness had always been and would continue to be part of him and because he was not easy to talk to, theirs would be a taciturn kind of companionship though never a shallow one. But now he knew what was beneath the dourness he would no longer be nervous in his presence.

Sandy was putting on his oilskins in the porch as Thomas approached him. 'If you're going to adopt me will I have to go on calling you Mr MacDonald?' he queried timidly.

Sandy paused. 'It doesn't sound too good, does it?' he conceded. 'What d'you think you should call me?' The door was open and Sandy stood with his back to Thomas, staring up at the rainbow which was beginning to thread itself through the thinning mist.

'I wish I c-could c-call you D-Dad,' responded Thomas, and was surprised at his own temerity.

Sandy did not turn round. 'I doubt you can do that,' he replied. Thomas's heart sank. 'You would only be able to call me D-D-Dad. . . . It would sound a bit daft.'

Thomas detected a teasing note in 'himself's' voice; the gentle kind of teasing that can draw two people into a deeper understanding of each other. He pretended to be stung by the taunt. 'I c-can. I c-can say it,' he insisted.

'Let's hear you, then.'

'D-D-Dad.' Thomas was furious with himself for stumbling over the word. 'D-Dad,' he tried again.

'I didn't think you could.' The teasing note was less evident but it was still there.

'Dad!' Thomas shouted the word assertively. 'Dad!' he repeated.

Sandy stood stiffly. He had been expecting that some day such a plea might be made and he had resolved in loyalty to Mairi that when it came he would not reject it, but despite that, his stern nature made him resist the sentimentality of the moment. It was several seconds before he could bring himself to speak.

'That sounds all right . . . son,' he said slowly. But still he did not turn to face Thomas. Whistling to Ben, he strode off up the hill.

Thomas moved to stand in the doorway and watch him go. 'Dad!' he whispered, and again, 'Dad!' and as his eyes followed Sandy, he saw the rainbow breaking through the mist to throw a strong arch of colour over the glen. Slowly the sadness that had drawn itself on the young face during the past few weeks was shaded away. The eyes lit with a glint of pride. Thomas found himself almost wishing it was a school day and imagined himself telling the other children, 'My Dad is giving me a puppy for my birthday. My Dad is taking me to the creels this afternoon. My Dad. . . .' He turned to look at the clock. His Dad had said he would be back in not much more than an hour. There would be time, Thomas reckoned.

Cutting himself another slice of the birthday cake, he pulled the door closed behind him and raced off in the direction of the shore, calling out to the seals as he ran and telling them of the new joy that was surging back into his life.

On the following pages are details of Arrow books that will be of interest.

THE HILLS IS LONELY

Lillian Beckwith

When Lillian Beckwith advertised for a quiet, secluded place in the country, she received the following unorthodox description of the attractions of life on an isolated Hebridean croft:

'Surely it's that quiet here even the sheeps themselves on the hills is lonely and as to the sea it's that near I use it myself every day for the refusals . . .'

Intrigued by her would-be landlady's letter and spurred on by the sceptism of her friends, Lillian Beckwith replied in the affirmative. THE HILLS IS LONELY is the hilarious and enchanting story of the extremely unusual rest cure that followed.

A BREATH OF BORDER AIR

Lavinia Derwent

'Looking back, I often wonder if any of it was real . . .'

Lavinia Derwent, well known as a best-selling author of children's books and as a television personality, here memorably portrays a childhood spent on a lonely farm in the Scottish Border country.

Here was an enchanted world of adventure: a world of wayward but endearing farm animals, and of local characters like Jock-the-herd . . . and Lavinia's closest friend, Jessie, who never failed to temper her earthy wisdom with a rare sense of humour.

'Any exiled Scot will breathe this fine air with joy' *Yorkshire Post*

ROCKS IN MY SCOTCH

Angus MacVicar

A fascinating and affectionate account of the author's boyhood and life in his beloved Mull of Kintyre where his father – the redoubtable Padre – was minister for forty-seven years. The vista widens, too, to Scotland as a whole to make a joyful mixture of anecdote, history, legend and reminiscence which is rich with the writer's love of his land and his people.

Angus MacVicar's stories range from the dramatic and tragic to the humorous and hilarious – and sometimes he is even a little annoyed with the modern world – but always they are a delight to read – again and again.

'Delightful' *Sunday Express*

BESTSELLING SCOTTISH BOOKS
FROM ARROW

All these books are available from your bookshop or news-agent or you can order them direct. Just tick the titles you want and complete the form below.

☐	A BREATH OF BORDER AIR	Lavinia Derwent	£1.25
☐	GOD BLESS THE BORDERS	Lavinia Derwent	£1.25
☐	LADY OF THE MANSE	Lavinia Derwent	£1.75
☐	ONE SMALL FOOTPRINT	Molly Weir	£1.25
☐	ROCKS IN MY SCOTCH	Angus MacVicar	£1.25
☐	BEES IN MY BONNET	Angus MacVicar	£1.75
☐	SILVER IN MY SPORRAN	Angus MacVicar	£1.75
☐	BRUACH BLEND	Lillian Beckwith	£1.60
☐	BEAUTIFUL JUST	Lillian Beckwith	£1.60
☐	LIGHTLY POACHED	Lillian Beckwith	£1.60
☐	GREEN HAND	Lillian Beckwith	£1.60
☐	THE HILLS IS LONELY	Lillian Beckwith	£1.60
☐	A ROPE – IN CASE	Lillian Beckwith	£1.60
☐	THE SEA FOR BREAKFAST	Lillian Beckwith	£1.60
☐	A SHINE OF RAINBOWS	Lillian Beckwith	£1.75

Postage _____

Total _____

ARROW BOOKS, BOOKSERVICE BY POST, PO BOX 29, DOUGLAS, ISLE OF MAN, BRITISH ISLES

Please enclose a cheque or postal order made out to Arrow Books Limited for the amount due including 15p per book for postage and packing for orders both within the UK and overseas.

Please print clearly

NAME ....

ADDRESS ....

....

Whilst every effort is made to keep prices down and to keep popular books in print, Arrow Books cannot guarantee that prices will be the same as those advertised here or that the books will be available.

A SHINE OF RAINBOWS

Eagerly Thomas began to stammer out about
seeing the rainbow but he heard the door of
the bedroom open and Sandy's footsteps
coming through to the kitchen. Trying to
hurry out the words before 'himself'
appeared, Thomas was reduced to jerky
inarticulateness. Frustrated, he described
with his hands the extent of the arc of the
rainbow, and from his gestures and the one or
two intelligible words he had managed to
utter, Mairi was quick to deduce what he was
trying to convey.

'You've already seen a rainbow? My! My!
Thomas, then I think that must have been a
special one come just to welcome you to
Corrie.' She spoke with a lilting confidence.
'Do you not think that is so?' she appealed to
Sandy as he came into the room.

'Aye, indeed,' Sandy supported obligingly.
He slanted a flinty smile at Thomas, but
Thomas was looking down at his feet and did
not see it.